Held
for
Ransom

Held for Ransom

The Kronholm Kidnapping

BY RUTH PETERMAN

Tyndale House Publishers, Inc.
Wheaton, Illinois
Coverdale House Publishers, Ltd.
London, England

Library of Congress Catalog Card Number 75-15028. ISBN 8423-1414-8, paper. Copyright © 1975 by Tyndale House Publishers, Inc.; Wheaton, Illinois 60187. All rights reserved. Second printing, August 1975. Printed in the United States of America.

To David

Foreword

Thou art coming to a King,
Large petitions with thee bring,
For His grace and power are such
None can ever ask too much.
> —John Newton

The words of this hymn came to me often during those long hours of my captivity. Since my release, God has been teaching me more about what they mean. We receive according to how we ask: ask God for great things and you get great things.

As you read this book, you will see that the last day of my captivity I became very specific in my prayer and God gave me what I asked for. God has shown me, since, that the significance of that request was not so much in what I asked for myself, as it was in my concern that the *world* needed to know about such a great God.

The world did indeed hear. The story was carried in this country, in Canada, Europe, and Japan. It's been called a "twentieth-century miracle."

Why, of all the people kidnapped, including persons of great political and social stature, was

I given the opportunity to tell millions over all major TV and radio networks about God's protection and care? I believe it was because God was answering my prayer—that the world might know he was a prayer-answering God.

The world also prayed. We still hear from people from every denomination, every faith, and many different countries, telling us how they prayed. When I think of the many times my name was presented to the God of the universe, I feel very small. But, thank God, no one is too small or unimportant to come to him.

To all of you who prayed, my deep and humble thanks.

Eunice Kronholm

Monday,
February 24,
1975

Eunice

Eunice Kronholm turned left from Birch Street onto 7th Avenue North. Snow and ice produced a scene in white—a Currier and Ives.

The road wound through the woods and plains until an olive-colored townhouse appeared off to the left. A slight shudder passed through her. They had said the place they were holding her was a townhouse "near where you live."

She was able to think about it now. For almost a year, she had forced her mind away from those terrible moments. Driving slowly toward her own home at Lino Lakes, she scanned the area for the unusual. Lake Reshanau on the right kept placid silence. The golf course on the left held no life. Beyond it was the wooded area. She now knew that from those ermine-clad trees, a year ago, two men had watched her house many times.

As she pulled into her driveway, she took in the entire area—the house, the garage, the tool shed.

She shut off the ignition and removed the key. Their German Shepherd jumped to her feet from

9

where she lay on the step and trotted toward the car, trembling with anticipation of a petting.

"Hi ya, Cuddles." Eunice smiled at the dog as she searched the area with her eyes. "You look like you're smiling at me. Is everything all right? Should I come out?"

With the key to the front door in her fingers, Eunice shoved open the car door and ran to the house, almost stumbling over Cuddles on the way.

She still took the same precautions whenever she arrived home alone. It had been almost a year, but she still had the pounding heart and the trembling fingers.

Friday, March 15, 1974

Eunice

Eunice leaned toward the mirror for a closer view of herself. Red rims around her blue eyes showed she had been ill. It was to be her first outing of the week, and it was, she thought wryly, a good thing it was to the beauty shop.

She briskly pulled a comb through her short red-gold hair. Her appointment was for 8:15. She had eaten a bigger breakfast than usual. Rarely did her schedule coincide with Gunnar's. As president of his bank, he often had breakfast meetings and left before Eunice got up. But this morning they had had bacon and eggs and toast. After asking the blessing Gunnar had said, "What time will you be back from the beauty shop?"

"Oh, a little before ten. Maybe ten o'clock."

"I'll call you then. And we'll go shopping for a rug this afternoon. But I have a luncheon appointment at the Minneapolis Athletic Club at noon."

"O.K. I told them at the carpet place we could both make it by two o'clock."

"Fine. I'll be there." He kissed her. "I'll see if the windows of your car need scraping. It's pretty cold."

"Oh, thank you, honey." Eunice had watched him put on his hat and coat. His posture always erect, his manner so sure. He had more hair than many men sixty years old, and hardly a line in his face. For her his eyes were always gentle.

Hurrying now, Eunice glanced at her watch. The family room looked bare. The new rug would really brighten things up. She wished she felt better. The prospect of being with Gunnar later in the day cheered her spirits.

Frost had again gathered on the windows of her gold '69 Buick Skylark. The radio had said it was 30 degrees with a northwest wind of 20 miles an hour. It seemed colder—maybe the wind-chill factor, or her own lowered resistance. Because she'd had the flu, Eunice had put on the warmest clothes in her wardrobe—a gray half-wool pants suit with double long sleeves and a leather coat. At the last minute she had decided to wear her lined boots, even though she knew at the beauty shop they much preferred that their customers wear shoes. "Those floors are cold," Eunice had said to herself.

She started her car and proceeded to scrape off the frost which had again gathered on her windshield. Light snow lay where the green grass would soon appear on the gentle hills.

Her mind went back a week. They had just finished their wonderful trip to Israel, Greece, and Rome. Minnesota was not the best state to come home to in the middle of March. Immediately upon their return, she had come down with the flu.

Eunice loved their home all the more for its tranquil isolation. It faced the golf course on the right and to the south of them was the lake. They had neighbors only on the east side. She had loved every day of the year and a half she had lived here with Gunnar.

She scraped the rear window, then opened the car door to throw in the scraper. Suddenly she heard scuffling behind her, rushing from the side and rear. She froze. Two men in black clothing and snowmobile masks appeared, only their eyes and mouths showing. The roots of her hair jerked in her scalp; the taste of fear rose from her tightened throat.

"Get in!" they commanded. She saw a gun.

Eunice screamed. They seized her. "Get in!" They were trying to push her into the back seat of her car.

Holding onto the top of the car and bracing her feet, she screamed again. "Help! Help!" Turning sharply, she wrested herself out of their grasp. One grabbed her again and pressed his hand over her mouth. She tried to bite it. The other man pulled her hands roughly behind her and tied them.

They pushed her into the back seat of her own car, forcing her to lie face down. One of them followed her in.

Eunice was trembling inside and out. "God, oh, God," she prayed. "Jesus, Jesus."

The other man had gotten into the front. Backing out now, he threw Eunice's long acrilan scarf into the back. "Blindfold her with this," he ordered in a rough voice, "and tie it on with that rope I gave you." There was a lot of scarf there to wind around and around her head, covering her eyes and nose. Eunice was grateful for it. It had been given to her by a family she dearly loved.

Her fear combined with her nasal congestion to make it almost impossible to breathe. Her words often spoken to students of nursing returned to her: "When you're scared—too scared to breathe—pant like a dog. It will relax you." She did this now.

"Wh-what d-do y-you w-want?" Her teeth chattered so badly she could hardly get the words out.

"Money."

"*Money?*"

"Just do what we tell ya. Lay down and stay down and you won't get hurt."

The man kept his arm over her, less firmly now. Eunice was shivering so hard she shook the car seat. Terror gripped her. *Kidnapped.* She could tell they were going south to Minnesota Highway 49.

They turned. Then they turned again. And again. They were on bumpy roads and going fast. Eunice lost all sense of direction.

"I've just had the flu. Would you please cover me up. I'm not over it yet. I don't want to get pneumonia."

He covered her with her own blanket which had been in her cars for twenty years. It had gone with her on picnics and to ball games. She had her own blanket and her own scarf.

"I'm having trouble breathing. Would you push this scarf up just a little?" He obliged.

"Where are we going?"

"Not too much further."

After traveling in circles and over bumpy roads for an hour or more, they drove into what appeared to be an open garage. "Now you'll get out."

They guided her a few feet over to a corner. "Easy now. You just stay here a few minutes." They made her sit down on the cold floor. Eunice heard the car back out. Soon a different sounding car pulled into the garage. It was backing in. For her. She felt her last link with home was disappearing. For a moment she worried about her car. When will I ever see it again? What shape will it be in? Then realization of her own immediate danger forced itself on her. She really was kidnapped.

Friday, Gunnar

From his desk at the Drover State Bank in South St. Paul, Gunnar Kronholm telephoned his sister-in-law. "Dorothy? Say Dorothy, is Eunice there, by any chance? She's not? No—well, I don't know what to think. See, she had an early hair appointment but expected to be home around ten. Here it's 11:30 and I still haven't been able to reach her. No, I didn't try the beauty shop. She's not been going to the same one all the time lately. She'd surely be through there by now anyway.

"Yeah, call Ruth, will you? I called Joyce and she hasn't seen her.

"The thing is, Dorothy, I have to be at a meeting here at the bank at two and that's when I was going to meet Eunice to look at rugs. I'd like to catch her before she goes clear out there. Yes, I thought too she might be shopping. But it isn't like her not to keep in touch if she changes her plans.

"I've canceled a luncheon appointment. I'm uneasy—I feel somehow I should keep trying to reach her. If she comes there, have her call me, will you? Thanks, Dorothy."

Gunnar hung up. To his secretary he said, "Betty, keep trying to get Eunice, will you? I'll be back in a half hour or so."

After a quick bite to eat, Gunnar called his neighbor. "Howard, I've a favor to ask of you. Eunice was going to meet me at two o'clock to look for a rug. Now I find I can't keep that appointment with her, but I can't get hold of her." After telling Howard of Eunice's morning plans and his previous efforts to locate her, Gunnar said, "I'm wondering if it would be too much to ask of you to please check the house. It just isn't like her not to keep in touch if she changes her plans."

Five minutes later, Howard called back. "Everything here looks O.K. The car's gone. Her dog's in the house. Sleeping on the rug in the kitchen, cute as a button, all right. Those Yorkshire terriers—"

"Howard, I'm more than a little uneasy about Eunice. Is there—does everything look normal? Is there any sign of—I mean—"

"No, everything seems normal to me. Knop

16

was perfectly relaxed on the rug. Your wife must have gone shopping or something, don't you think?"

"Probably did. Thanks an awful lot, Howard."

He had to call the carpet place. Globe Furniture Company. Yes, they were expecting Mrs. Kronholm at two o'clock. "This is her husband. I was supposed to meet her there. Now I find that I am unable to come. Would you please have her call me when she gets there? Thank you."

Friday, Eunice

The car was backing into the garage. She really and truly was kidnapped. "Oh, what will they do with me?" They helped her into the car. The seat seemed higher than most cars. Was it a van? The seat wasn't hard plastic material, but it all seemed different.

"Lay down and be quiet."

"What—are—you going to do—with—me —now?" Fear nauseated her.

"We'll tell you when we get there. Just lay down. You cooperate and be quiet and nothing's going to happen to you."

"Jesus, Jesus."

Thou wilt keep him in perfect peace whose mind is stayed on thee.

A deep sense of peace came over her. God had not forsaken her. He knew where she was.

It seemed to Eunice they were traveling the same bumpy route they had just come. It felt as though they were up on gutter curbs and down. She had no idea where they were.

Eunice had to think. A nurse with a master's degree in psychology, she had for many years counseled and taught in schools of nursing. If this were a problem a student had, what advice would Eunice give her?

"Try to determine what is the worst possible thing that could happen to you," she had often told them. "When you have decided what that would be, try to accept that. If you have accepted the worst possibility, you will be able to accept every other development."

Could she apply this to herself? She was kidnapped. For a ransom. What was the worst thing she feared? Death. Eunice had taught courses on death and dying. Now the word arose out of her vocabulary like a new word. One she had never used before. Now she was talking about the death of Eunice Kronholm.

"Me. Dead. The end of my existence in this world. The end of my thoughts and desires. The period at the end of the sentence which is me." Could she accept that?

How would it come? Would it be quick? Would they torture her? The gun. The man who had ridden in the back with her in her own car hadn't spoken for a long time. Where was he? The other one, the driver, he seemed rougher. Was the gun in the front seat with him? Was he taking her out to the country somewhere to do away with her?

Eunice wanted to live. She had come into a good full and happy life. She had always loved life, but these last few years married to Gunnar had been the epitome of joy. She had never known such happiness. No, she wouldn't accept death.

Perhaps for herself, she could accept death. But could Gunnar go through such anguish again? Life had ended for him once before as he had stood with six adolescent children and young adults over the grave of his first wife. Then he had loved again. Eunice had joyously taken him and his family to her heart. She loved them all and they loved her.

If she were killed, Gunnar would be alone again. How could he go back to his banking business knowing Eunice had lost her life because of his position as president? No, he would be devastated. His children were all grown now. He was more alone than when she had married him. She had to live for his sake. And she dearly wanted to live.

But what if it comes to that? What if they do kill you? The question persisted.

"God, you know I'm ready to die. You know I love life and love my family. You know all about Gunnar and his needs. You took care of him before I ever married him, and I know you can continue to do so. God, I give it all to you. If I must die—if this is your will for me, my Father, I beg you to be everything to Gunnar that he will need. Yes, I give it to you. I would accept death."

God's presence overwhelmed her in a Shekinah-like glory. Goose bumps broke out all over her body. God had sealed her decision and she was at peace.

The car was stopping. What would it be? He could drown her in a lake or shoot her and bury her. Eunice started to tremble again. She heard a garage door open with a metallic, grinding sound. The car drove in. There was no other sound anywhere. The car door opened and someone took her arm. He guided her up a few steps and into a room of some sort. "Sit down here." The chair was hard, like a kitchen chair. The room seemed darkened. "You can lay down if you want."

Since no bed was indicated, Eunice supposed he meant the floor. From under her blindfold, she could see a white shag rug on the floor. She had her blanket. The man untied her hands and covered her up.

"H-how long are we going to be here?"

"You should be home in a few hours if everyone cooperates."

"Why did you pick me?"

"We picked you and your husband at random. We had planned to take him too, but he got away too early this morning. We would've dropped him off at the bank and told him what to do. But we bungled it, so now we have to start over."

So that was it. "Did you just pick our name out of a hat?"

"Out of a directory. Now be quiet. I don't want you to talk!"

He sounded cross. "We'll have to wait here until we get the money."

"When will that be?"

"Well, whenever we can reach your husband at the bank."

Eunice sat right up. "Well, you better get going then. He's not the easiest man to reach."

"It's out of our hands."

"What do you mean?"

"The other guys are handling that end of it."

"What other guys?"

"A coupla other fellows are doing the negotiating. We just have to wait. The other fellows are from around here; I'm not."

"What time is it?"

"Eleven o'clock. Now be quiet."

Eunice wondered if the other men had been able to reach Gunnar. He had a luncheon appointment with someone. She hoped they had caught him at the bank before he left. Poor Gunnar. He'd be beside himself with worry. Even as her thoughts went to him she prayed, "O God, help him to stay calm and to know what to do."

Her captor was speaking again. "This all was s'posed to take only a few hours. We were going to pick up you and your husband. But we bungled it. We were going to tell him we'd release you when we got the money. Then we let him get away. How come you didn't go to work together?"

"We never do."

"Well, you work at the bank, dontcha?"

"No, I've never worked at the bank. I'm a nurse."

"A nurse?"

"Yes, I've worked many places. After I got my degree, I worked in an operating room for some time. I've been in charge of the health services at Bethel College for four years. I taught medical

21

and surgical nursing at Fairview, also psychiatric nursing. Same at Northwestern. Then I
went into counseling. No, I've never worked at
the bank."

"You never worked at the bank? Well, do you
have a daughter that works at the bank?"

"The girls have worked there."

"Well, is one of them named after you?"

"No, neither one of them is 'Eunice.' " Didn't
the man even know she was not the girls'
mother?

"Well, I'll be darned. You're lucky though.
You're lucky it's me and not those other guys
you're with. One of them—wow—he must be a
sadist. He'd have to be to do some of the things
he does. Course, I'm not such a good guy either. I
sometimes think I should see a psychiatrist myself. I can be pretty ugly."

Eunice shivered. He moved around the room
and from underneath her blindfold from where
she lay, Eunice caught a glimpse of her abductor
in front of a mirror. For a moment she saw a
rather young face, even features, brown hair.
Probably in his thirties.

She could tell there was one window in the
room, with a mattress pad over it for a shade.
The pad had red trimming.

"I'm having trouble breathing. Would you
please push this scarf up?"

He did so. "That's a beautiful diamond you're
wearing."

"Thank you. It's my engagement ring."

"How big is it? Do you know?"

"Not quite a carat." Eunice tucked the ringed

finger under her blanket. Was this merely to make conversation, or would he take it?

"It's beautiful."

"Thank you. Yes, it is."

In the silence that fell between them, her thoughts returned to her days of courtship. She had known Gunnar all her life and from time to time had heard news about him and his family. She had known his first wife and had learned of her death.

Eunice's sister Ruth had visited in Gunnar's home while she went to college. Ruth had commented on what a fine man Gunnar was. After his wife died, Ruth and Emmett Johnson, a minister friend Eunice had known from childhood, both mentioned Gunnar to Eunice and suggested they would make a good match. Eunice listened with good humor and mild interest.

She had dated regularly through the years, always considering the possibility that one day she might marry. When she had been much younger, before she was twenty, she had prayed that God would lead her into marriage with a man who would love God more than her.

In January of 1970, Emmett Johnson arranged with the consent of both Eunice and Gunnar to have them meet the Johnsons for dinner. They went to a good restaurant and spent the time bringing each other up to date on their own lives and discussing mutual acquaintances. After dinner, they went to see Gunnar's youngest son Mark, then a senior in high school, play hockey.

When they said "goodnight," Eunice secretly hoped Gunnar would ask her out again. She didn't have long to wait. They had several dates that winter and spring.

In June, Eunice went to the Orient and learned upon her return that Gunnar had tried to locate her. They had a date in August.

Eunice now remembered a date when she had had a bad cold. Try as she would, she couldn't enjoy the evening. It had been very dull. Realizing she had contributed so little to the evening, she resolved to call Gunnar when she felt better.

She did this, and it seemed to give Gunnar the encouragment he had needed. From then on, he seemed freer with her and more aggressive in pursuing their relationship. She returned the interest. He had the qualities she would like in a husband.

They went for many walks that fall just to get to know each other better. One day in particular returned to her now: the day they went hiking together in the north woods, near Chisholm. It was a fall day, such as God makes only for lovers. The sun shone just for them. The birds sang just for them. The birch trees seemed to have risen to their great height just for them and stood silent witnesses to their love. They laughed and sang and talked as they crunched through the leaves of red and gold, fallen from the maples.

Never had they felt so close, so intimate, so free. Tears came into Eunice's eyes as she relived those tender moments when she had gone into Gunnar's arms as though she belonged there—as though she were born to be there. She felt again the strength of his chest and arms. She heard him whispering, "I love you." It seemed he were saying it now: "I love you." It was as if he were saying, "Because I love you, you will be safe. I am building a fortress around you with my love and prayers."

They were married February 27, 1971, in the chapel at Bethlehem Baptist Church. Gunnar's brother-in-law, Bruce Fleming, had performed the ceremony, assisted by the man who had arranged their first date—Emmett Johnson. Gunnar's son John stood up with him and Mabel Peterson from Connecticut stood up with Eunice. Close friends and relatives rounded out the number to about a hundred.

They had honeymooned at Lutsen's resort on the north shore of Lake Superior. Gunnar, who had never skied before, broke in a ski outfit Eunice had given him for Christmas. They had laughed at his manly efforts to stay on his feet. The whole first day, he had done nothing but fall. The second day, staying upright became easier and the third day he skied without an instructor's aid and fell hardly at all.

Remembering those precious five days and nights, her heart almost burst with love and longing for Gunnar. Tears moistened the blindfold and hard-to-swallow lumps kept coming into her throat.

Her captor had made no effort to take the ring. She kept it hidden, hoping he wouldn't talk about it anymore.

Eunice's bowels were churning angrily. Would they trust her to be alone? She had to ask. "I would like to use the bathroom."

She felt his arm. His shirt sleeve was of soft

material. He guided her through a hallway. "Here's the top of the tank. O.K.?"

"Fine, thank you." He had left her but had not closed the door. Should she close it? She didn't dare. Again her training in psychology came to her. She refused to make this her problem, recognizing that the man had a problem if he chose to put her through the embarrassment of using the toilet without privacy.

When she had finished, he met her at the door. "Where's the other fellow that was here this morning?"

'He'll be back pretty soon."

Eunice hoped he was getting the money. "I'm thirsty. Do you suppose I could have a drink of water?"

He seemed to have to walk through several rooms. He brought her a cup of water.

"Thank you. Uh—since I don't know your name, would it be all right if I made one up for you? Why don't I just call you Bill?"

"That's fine with me." Bill walked about restlessly.

"Good. Now I don't feel as though I'm talking to the wall. Are you married?"

"Yeah."

"Bill, you seem to be basically a good fellow. How did you ever let yourself get into this mess?"

"Well, I needed money."

"But money doesn't assure happiness. There is much more to life than that."

"I-I can't figure you out. You're—so calm. And I'm—so nervous."

"Well, if I'm calm it's because I'm in a right relationship to God. I feel strongly he's in control of the situation I'm in and will take care of me. Even if I'm scared I really have peace in my heart. Do you want to hear more about it?"

"Yeah. Yes, I would."

Bill sat down on the floor next to Eunice and they sat like two friends on a rug in a family room. Eunice said, "Well, many years ago, I found out who God was and what he wants to do for people—for me. He wanted happiness for me more than I wanted it for myself. All he wanted was for me to allow him to control my life. He wanted me to believe that he loved me so much that he sent his Son, the Lord Jesus, to show us how to live and love other people. In fact, he loved us so much that he allowed his Son to die for our sins. Now all we have to do is accept that fact and ask God to forgive us our sins and take our lives and make us into the kinds of people he wants us to be."

"Sounds easy."

"Well, it is—that's why it's for anybody."

Silence fell between them. Bill made no comments. Eunice prayed, "O God, work in his heart. Even through this may he come to know you."

After a few moments, Eunice said, "You say you're married. Do you have children?"

"Yeah—ah—I don't want to tell you about myself."

"O.K."

He left her alone in the room. Where is this place, she wondered. The house was carpeted, but there was no furniture. It seemed heated, but was not lived in. How strange.

Morning passed to afternoon. No one spoke of lunch. Eunice's sinuses had been draining heavily all morning. With each trip to the bathroom, she had been taking back with her large quantities of tissue.

She was getting hungry. She had left the house well fortified, but that seemed long ago. When she was nervous and hungry at the same time, she tended to have ulcer-like pains in her stomach. She knew it could be disastrous for her to do without food too long. She drank all the water she could just to keep something inside her.

Surely the Lord knew about this too. As her tension mounted and her stomach distress increased, she remembered "Thou wilt keep him in perfect peace whose mind is stayed on thee."

"God," she prayed, "help me to relax. Help me not to feel the hunger. Help me not to get sick." She felt that if her Father could see to it that she came into this day with a big breakfast, he could and would look after her in everything else too.

Suddenly, she remembered what a doctor had once told her. He said the mucus drained from the sinuses was protein and if swallowed would be digested and used by the body. Now she decided to make that mucus work for her. She swallowed all of it. Before long, her hunger pangs were relieved. Truly, if her loving Father would oversee her in the details of food and a nervous stomach, he would also protect her in such an enormity as a kidnapping.

She became aware of what sounded like a dispatcher radio coming from another room. Bill came in. "Well, we didn't get hold of your husband. Do you know any place he might be?"

"Only that he was going to the Minneapolis Athletic Club for lunch. Why don't you call him there? And he was going to the Globe carpet place at two o'clock. We were going to look for a rug. I was supposed to meet him there. If he doesn't know yet that I'm missing, he'll know it when I don't show up."

"Oh, we'd better get over there then."

"What time is it?"

"A little after one."

"Oh, my yes, you'd better."

Bill was gone too short a time. "There's no such place. We couldn't find it."

He couldn't have gone anywhere himself. Was he in touch with the other man, or the other men? Eunice raised herself on an elbow. "Of course, there's such a place. It must be listed in the phone book."

What had gone wrong? She said, "You know—there's no way you can get money after 3:30. There's an automatic closure of the vault and the banks aren't open Saturday and Sunday, you know."

"Guess we'll have to stay here all night. There's no way we could get the money anymore now. We sure made a mess of this thing." He paced up and down. "Really blew it."

Eunice heard the radio in the next room. "Go

to . . ." "Eagan," "Corner of . . ."—a word here and there.

Bill said, "One of the other fellows in on this is a former policeman. That's how we got this police radio." He paced back and forth. "Man, we sure bungled this thing."

Friday,
Gunnar

The Discount Committee meeting commenced promptly at two o'clock in Gunnar's office. There were many loans to review that day.

Gunnar fidgeted in his chair. A deep sense of foreboding hung over him. "Would you recommend that we pass this one by for the time being, Gunnar? Gunnar?"

He jerked back to the present. He had to force himself to concentrate. Twice he slipped out to ask Betty if she had learned anything about Eunice. Where could she be?

At 3:40, Betty appeared in the doorway with uncertainty and apprehension on her face. Gunnar half rose from his chair then sat down. She spoke in a low voice. "Mr. Kronholm, I know you didn't want to take calls, but there's a man on the phone who insists on talking to you. I told him you were in conference, but he says it's urgent."

Gunnar excused himself and followed her to her desk. "Gunnar Kronholm speaking."

A breathy voice spoke. "We have your wife.

Get all the money you can and deliver it to a station—"

Cold sweat broke out from every pore. Gunnar's legs went weak. He leaned on the desk. "Would you kindly repeat that, please?"

The receiver went dead.

"Please, please, would you repeat the instructions?"

The caller had hung up. With wooden feet, Gunnar found his way back to the committee. He went to his desk and held onto it with both hands. In a thin voice, he said, "Gentlemen, I have a problem."

Absorbed in their discussion, the men paid no attention to him. He forced his voice through a dry throat and lips that weren't his own. "Gentlemen, I have a problem. Eunice has been kidnapped."

At that point, the vice-president of the bank saw him. "Fellows, something's wrong here. Gunnar's got something to tell us."

Still hanging onto his desk, Gunnar repeated, "Eunice has been kidnapped."

Everyone froze. There was a moment of silence then confusion broke out. Everyone talked. They were running in all directions.

Still standing at his desk, Gunnar took charge. "Will you get Bob Anderson in here, please?"

Anderson, the security officer of the bank, came in. "Bob, Eunice has been kidnapped. I had a call from her abductors. Get in touch with the FBI."

His face registering shock, Bob seated himself in Gunnar's chair and started looking through

31

the phone book. Other members of the Board of Directors tried to help.

"Call the operator and ask for the FBI," Gunnar said. Soon they had the St. Paul office. They gave an agent the description of Eunice: five feet, five inches tall, 135 pounds, gold hair, blue eyes, age forty-six; and of her car: gold '69 Buick Skylark. The FBI asked for and got numbers of friends and relatives they could question regarding her possible whereabouts.

Gunnar finally sat down in his chair at his desk. There was so much that had to be done.

Had he built up the banking business for thirty-seven years for this? To have his wife taken by force for a ransom? "Dear God," he cried. "How could you let this happen? We've tried—we've tried to serve you in all the areas we've been given abilities in." Sobs wracked his chest. "We've gone through so much heartache before. Then you let me have Eunice. Dear God, how can you do this? How *can* you do this to me?"

Betty approached him. "Mr. Kronholm, Eunice's sister is on the line."

Ruth was in tears. "Gunnar, I had a call from the FBI. Do you know what they said? They think Eunice has been kidnapped."

Gunnar told her of his phone call from the abductor, himself holding back sobs. "No, No!" Ruth cried. They tried to console each other, finally agreeing that all they could do was pray.

Once more, Gunnar returned to his thoughts. His mind went back to his life before Eunice. He recalled when Elna, his first wife, had gotten the news that she had cancer. In direct answer to her specific prayer, God had added thirteen years to her life in order that she might help raise the children, at the time ranging in age from two to twelve years. Those years had been happy but hard. Always hanging over them was the knowledge that the disease would ultimately claim her. Pain and suffering and tension took turns with relief, merriment, and relaxation. Then the inevitable had become fact. He had lost her. As he remembered now that deep sense of loss and this present threat his thought was, "Curse God and die."

Death had taken his mother from him at an early age. The second eldest of five children, Gunnar had had to help his father hold the family together. Now he felt like putting his head down on his arms and crying like that little boy. But he couldn't fall apart. Things had to be done.

Could he go through whatever he might have to endure? Torturous thoughts shot through his mind. Eunice molested. Eunice tortured. Never hearing from her again. Finding her bludgeoned body.

A man was being led to his desk. He showed his card, "Bill Lais of the FBI." They shook hands. "We're going to station some men around the bank. I don't expect the abductors will try anything around here, but we'd better be prepared. Since they have already referred to money, it would be well for you to make arrangements at once for ransom payment."

"The Chairman of our Board is here—" Turn-

ing to him and the Director representing the
Majority Stockholder, Gunnar said, "I don't
know what they're going to be asking, but you
men are going to have to instruct and advise the
officers of our bank so that when the demand
comes we can make whatever arrangements are
necessary to meet their demands."

There was so much to do. He couldn't give
up—yet.

Friday,
Eunice

Bill opened the door to let someone
in. Eunice heard two voices. Bill sounded dis-
gusted. "Bungled it" reached her ears. She
strained to hear more. The police radio was
chattering away. At times Bill's voice rose.

Her bowels rolled and rumbled. She dreaded
a repeat of her earlier embarrassment. But she
had to call. "Please, could I go to the bathroom?"

"Sure. Here." She felt a hand. This time it was
the voice of the other fellow. For some reason,
she had less fear of him. She hoped he would
close the bathroom door.

He did. Eunice didn't know if she'd ever have
a chance to describe this house they were keeping her in, but she did her best to see from under
the blindfold. The bathroom had cream tiling
with brown stripes inside a hexagon shape inside a square. Little chandeliers lighted the mirror over the sink. The woodwork was dark oak as

was the vanity. The tub and stool were cream colored.

She opened the door. As her hand touched his, Eunice said, "I don't know your name but I gave the other fellow the name Bill so I wouldn't have to talk to the wall all the time. What do you want me to call you?"

"Just call me Jerry."

"O. K., Jerry."

From the unrest of her bowels, Eunice knew her diarrhea was not over. "Jerry," she said, "I guess it's because I'm nervous, but I have to go to the bathroom a lot."

"Yeah, gosh, that's too bad. Too bad this had to happen to you." He left for a moment, saying something about "Bubble-up."

Bill burst into the room. "There's police all over the place. One's been shot—"

"Oh, no!" Eunice sat up at once. "How did that ever happen? What did they do that for? How's this going to end?"

"Now don't you get all excited."

"What happened?"

"One of our guys probably went through a light or something, I don't know, and got nervous." Eunice remembered the shiny gun they had held on her when she was taken. Bill added, "The cop probably stopped him and our man got nervous and shot him."

"Was he badly hurt?"

"They don't know yet."

Fear gnawed at Eunice. If they were really that nervous anything could happen.

Jerry returned with a can of Bubble-up and a

35

two-inch slice of a submarine sandwich. "Maybe this will settle your insides."

"Thank you, Jerry. Thanks a lot." It had ham and cheese. Eunice withdrew into her thoughts. She yearned for Gunnar. What a state he must be in by this time! He would have gone to the rug place. He would telephone the house and the beauty shop. What would he think when he learned she hadn't kept her hair appointment. He'd call his sister-in-law, Dorothy, and Eunice's sister Ruth Berg.

Hadn't these men talked to Gunnar at all yet? What about the "others" in the case? It didn't seem the time to try to get information from Bill. Maybe later Jerry would tell her something.

It was late afternoon. She lay there in utter despair. Nobody knew where she was. She was at the mercy of men growing increasingly nervous about a bungled job.

My help comes from the Lord. He who keepeth thee will not slumber. Behold, he who keepeth Israel will neither slumber nor sleep. The Lord will preserve thee from all evil. He shall preserve thy soul. The Lord shall preserve thy going out and thy coming in . . .

The words had come to her right out of heaven. She would get home safely.

She prickled with emotion. The Lord was here. She was not alone. Tears came into her eyes. Had he not said, "I will never leave you nor forsake you?" No matter what the outcome, he would be with her. And with Gunnar. "Lord, will you please assure him that I'm all right? Help him to be able to get the money fast and get me out of here. Does he even know yet that they want money?" Her thoughts went around and around.

Jerry had been out for a few minutes. Now he returned. "The percolator don't work too good, but it's coffee anyway." He took her hand. "It's pretty hot. Careful."

"I thought I smelled coffee." She sat up. "Boy, that's good. Really hits the spot." She sipped it. It trickled right down to where her hunger was. "I've been wondering—do you have any idea—whatever happened to my car? How are you going to get rid of that?"

"We took care of it." She could tell he was grinning. "At least you'll get a new car out of it."

"What? You mean you wrecked it?"

"No, no. I mean by the time the FBI are through with it. They'll find it and pry open the trunk and—"

"And it won't be much good after that, will it?"

"I don't understand you," Jerry said. "You stay so calm. How can you stay so calm?"

"Jerry, it isn't myself. I'd be very upset if I weren't a Christian. I feel God is taking care of me." She paused a moment, then, "I feel sorry for you, Jerry, that you got into this kind of thing to make money in this way. Money doesn't guarantee happiness. I became a Christian by accepting Christ as my Savior. Would you like me to tell you more about it?"

"No! No, I don't want to hear any more about it."

"All right then, we'll talk about something

else." Sipping her coffee, Eunice wondered where Jerry had developed such an antipathy for the gospel. His sharp rejection surprised her.

Bill came in. "We'll have to spend the night here. Here's another blanket and a pillow."

"What are you going to do?"

"Stay here. What else is there to do?"

Eunice guessed he was right. Nothing was happening for her release. She lay down. One of them, she figured it was Bill, was making a bed in the same room. It seemed he was planning to sleep in front of the door.

Friday,
Gunnar

Relatives who lived in the area and friends who were allowed through the FBI blockade, had gathered at the Kronholm residence to pray and wait. Gunnar's brother Oliver and his wife Dorothy were there, as were his sister Astrid and her husband the Rev. Bruce Fleming, pastor of Bethlehem Baptist Church in Minneapolis. Gunnar's oldest child, John, and his wife Jan had come right over. And there was Jim Holm, Gunnar's 25-year-old nephew whom Gunnar lovingly called his "fourth son." Joyce Johannessen, a long-time friend of Eunice, had organized the ladies, and the dining room table was laden with breads, cheeses, cold cuts, and hot dishes sent over by neighbors.

The one fragmentary message was the only word Gunnar had received from the kidnappers. The man had sounded too distraught to know what he was about, which had increased Gunnar's alarm.

The FBI had set up a receiving station in the master bedroom. "You'll get all the news about your wife as it comes over the wires." Not much was coming in, but the family crowded around it. They sat on the bed and on the floor, listening and waiting. Two FBI agents, Clay Brady and Bob Harvey, had been stationed in the home.

The hours passed. This bedroom, the room Gunnar shared with Eunice, was full of her precious belongings. His eyes went from the silk etchings she had received from her brother when he was in Germany to the Japanese block prints over the bed.

He wandered out of the bedroom through the house. Would she ever return to live in this house with him again? He dropped into a chair at the far end of the living room, from which he had the full view of the dining room. Several other members of the family sat here and there in thought and prayer.

He gave himself up to memories. Thoughts of Eunice forced out all the others. The smell of her hair, the warmth of her body—her strong voice and hearty laugh—her quick hugs and impetuous squeezes. "Oh, God, dear dear God." Sobs shook his frame. "I beg of you, don't, *don't* let those men touch her. Keep her safe. Keep her well. Don't let her flu get worse. God, my Father, don't let those men torture her. I beg of you, don't let them touch her. May we soon hear. Let contact be made. May the demands be such that we can meet them."

Jim Holm came through the room just then. Seeing Gunnar's distress, he put his arms around him and they wept together. "Uncle Gunnar, she's going to be all right." Gunnar couldn't answer.

The night wore on. Gunnar went to the bedroom and listened to the FBI radio from time to time. Restless, he would walk about the house.

Clay Brady approached him. "Perhaps you should think about some kind of statement you could give the press in the morning."

"What can we say? We've heard nothing to speak of."

"Well, you might say that then. You might issue a plea to the kidnappers to make contact."

"That's a thought."

"Why don't you and your brother and the minister here, ah—"

"Bruce. Bruce Fleming."

"Yeah, why don't you go by yourselves and pray about it?"

What a fine man Clay was. Gunnar pondered the mercy, the kindness of God to provide Christian FBI men to counsel them in these trying hours.

The men prayed together and agreed upon a message for the press which they would give at nine o'clock the next morning.

Friday, Eunice

Eunice slept very little. She wrestled with the possibilities. Conflict twice resolved

40

during the day rose up again to torment her. "God, you could have spared us all this. Why did you remove the hedge? If you can protect me, why didn't you prevent this?" Did God cause this to happen; did he even allow it? Her theology balked at the idea. "God, I can't believe it of you. If you allowed it, I can't imagine why. Haven't I always trusted you? Hasn't Gunnar? What worse thing could have happened to us than this? Have we trusted you for nothing?" Her pulse hammered at her ears. Her heart pounded in thick surges.

There was no answer by whirlwind or tempest. Simply God answered her from his mind to hers, "I never promised to keep you from all trials, but I have promised that I will give you the grace and strength to bear it. Fear thou not for I am with thee. Be not dismayed for I am thy God."

Once again, she stood on the site where Paul had been a prisoner of the Lord Jesus Christ. Was it really only a week and a half ago they had been in Rome? It seemed as though that had happened to someone else. Paul's faith in God had never wavered. And in the Philippian jail, he and Silas had sung hymns in praise to God at midnight. Oh, that she might keep such a steadfast faith.

Her thoughts kept turning back to that terrible moment when she had been forcibly taken from her home, but she couldn't allow her mind to return to that experience. It was too dreadful. Each time she found herself driven to remembering the events of those few minutes, she consciously and with great power of will turned back to Scripture. She had taught her nursing students that one can control his mind. Now she had to do it.

With Bill lying at the door, all chance of escape was gone. Besides, if they should catch her trying to get away, they might be harder on her. So far, they had brought her water whenever she asked for it and food when they had it. She had blankets and even a pillow. They willingly helped her adjust her scarf when it shut off her breathing and they took her to the bathroom.

No, she would stay where she was. Things could be a lot worse.

Saturday,
March 16,
The Bergs

The task of telling Eunice's mother about the kidnapping fell to Eunice's sister Ruth and her husband, Wally Berg. Marie Peterson, 88 years old, lived in the Grandview Nursing Home at Cambridge, Minnesota, an hour's drive from the Twin Cities. Here also lived the aged father of Gunnar Kronholm, who would have to be told of this most recent tragedy in his son's life.

After a sleepless night filled with prayer in which she claimed God's promises of protection and safety for Eunice, Ruth rose at six o'clock. Almost immediately she telephoned the nursing home. The administrator there was Rev. Orville Johnson, long-time personal friend, former neighbor and pastor of the Petersons, dating back to their years at Chisholm, Minnesota.

After telling him about Eunice, Ruth said, "So, would you please sort of stay around Mother this morning until I can get there? See if you can spare her from hearing this from somebody. It will surely be in the paper this morning; it may have been on the air already."

Mrs. Peterson had been planning to spend the weekend in St. Paul with her daughters so she had made an 8:30 appointment with the hair dresser at the Home. Eunice and Gunnar were going to come to get her.

When Ruth and Wally walked in about 8:30, Mrs. Peterson expressed surprise. In her heavy Scandinavian accent she said, "So you came instead. Isn't it lucky I'm ready? Do you know that Sophie Lufie here let me go ahead of her, odervise I vouldn't be ready yet. She insisted that I go ahead of her. So, let's go to my room and get my tings."

As they walked slowly down the hall, Mrs. Peterson, leaning on her cane, cheerfully remarked, "Dey gafe me da red carpet treatment today. I efen got breakfast under da drier, can you beat dat? I nefer expected anyting like dat!"

Ruth saw that Pastor Johnson had pledged the other members of the home to secrecy about the kidnapping. Mrs. Lufie had given up her slot for having her hair done and they had brought Mrs. Peterson her breakfast in the beauty shop to keep her from going to the dining room where someone just might let slip the news about Eunice.

"So where's Euny?"

Ruth gulped. She didn't want to tell her in the hall. "Oh, I don't know." She tried to be casual.

They had come to Mrs. Peterson's room. An aide would be bringing Ed Kronholm down in his wheel chair. Both the Johnsons lingered about in the background. Ruth couldn't put it off. The moment had come. Her mother had to be told.

"Mom, I have something to tell you." She looked into her mother's blue-gray eyes, slightly sunken now, thinking, "No woman who has lived so long should have to hear such news."

Mrs. Peterson turned and looked questioningly into her daughter's face. Ruth's voice had trembled. Her eyes glistened with tears held back. "Well, so, what's da matter?"

"Mom, it's something about Euny." She gave her mother time to imagine the worst. Let her think accident—or death. It would only partly prepare her for this monstrous thing. "Euny's been kidnapped."

"KIDNAPPED!" She let out a scream then crumpled. "Kidnapped!" she cried again and sobbed, her shoulders shaking. "Euny Euny Euny." The mother wept over her youngest like David for his son Absalom. Ruth held her mother in her arms, both of them weeping.

Immediately, Pastor Johnson and his wife threw their arms around them both and began to cry out to God. "O God, we know you know what's happening to Eunice and will take care of her. We thank you that you know where she is and we believe you will keep her safe. O God, keep her safe—keep her from all harm. Father, we pray that you will get the glory. Give all these dear family members strength to stand. We know you hear us when we pray."

Ed Kronholm was wheeled into the room. Ruth looked at him. Though he was two years younger than Mrs. Peterson, his face, deep wrinkles lying upon one another as though vying for space, could best be described as ancient—weathered as much from hardship as from the elements. His wispy gray hair had been

45

neatly combed. His wise old eyes, always ready
to glimmer with amusement, now appeared to
be taking in the situation.

Ruth told him. He made no sound. He sat still
in his chair. That he had comprehended, Ruth
had no doubt. His face had drained of all color.
His eyes slowly left Ruth's and moved to his old
friend of seventy years. They had each had their
share of knocks. Now she was left—and he was
left. Left to endure one more test. He put out a
trembling hand. Mrs. Peterson took it. He
covered it with his other hand and they both
wept.

"It's—terrible. *Terrible*," he said. "Poor Gunnar. Poor Eunice."

Once more the Johnsons prayed with them
all. Mr. Kronholm squeezed Mrs. Peterson's
hand in a wordless, anguished farewell and was
wheeled from the room.

Because Mrs. Peterson had a heart condition,
the doctor felt she should have a sedative. They
helped her to the car and she dozed most of the
way to St. Paul.

Saturday, Eunice

Morning finally came. Jerry brought
her coffee. "This percolator just don't work
right."

"Well, it'll sure taste good anyway."

Bill said, "When you're through with your
coffee, you can take that scarf off and wash up in
the bathroom if you want. Then I'll put a different blindfold on you."

Eunice jumped up. "Oh, good. I'm through."

"That is, if you promise not to look around too much. I don't want you to know everything about this place if you ever have to identify it."

"O.K., I won't." Eunice had seen all she cared to from underneath the scarf on Friday. She had memorized every detail possible, so she didn't have to look about her at all.

How good it seemed to wash. She scrubbed her face and neck and ears. She ran water over her wrists. She rinsed with cold. Things seemed better after she had cleaned her mouth and rubbed her face. She enjoyed seeing again and opened and shut her eyes for the sheer pleasure of it. Her reflection in the mirror made her wince. Never had she looked so unkempt. She ran her fingers through her matted hair, relieved to be rid of the heavy scarf at last.

As she dried her hands, she noted a black hair on her sleeve. She put it in her billfold. While she had it open, she checked to see if her money was still there. It was. Six dollars in bills. "If they should take my money—I wonder—" She decided to put a dime in her cosmetic case, just in case they should let her go and she'd want to make a phone call.

When she came out, she kept her eyes shut until Bill had taped a piece of gauze firmly over them with surgical tape. It was pretty tight, but Eunice opened her eyes as far as she could under the blindfold. She had heard that horses go blind after being down in mines a long time. She wasn't about to lose her sight from lack of use of her eyes.

47

Either Bill or Jerry stayed with Eunice all of the time. Eunice lost track of time. She realized that her stomach was comfortable. It had been ever since she had started swallowing all of that mucus.

"Well, what shall we talk about?" she asked. Jerry seemed to welcome conversation. Eunice marveled at the way these men responded when she practiced the psychology she taught. People do need people. Jerry was under as much tension as she was, and talking relieved them both.

"Do you have a family, Jerry?"

"Yeah. I've got kids. I'm divorced."

"Is that so? You aren't from around here, you say?"

"No, well, I was raised in the South."

"Tell me about it. What was your mother like?"

"Too good for my dad, that's for sure. He drank and got pretty mean to my mother."

"Jerry, you've been kind to me and I appreciate it. You seem to have a rather high opinion of women."

"I guess that's right. Yeah, I sort of do have women on a pretty high pedestal. I never saw a woman like you before though. You're not scared. Some women would be crying and hollering. I'm sure glad you're not."

"I can't take the credit for that, Jerry. I told you why that is."

"Yeah."

"I had a good mother, too, Jerry. She's still living." With a pang Eunice thought of her mother. Had the family told her the bad news?

They would have to. Jerry was talking again.

"Ma and I used to love shrimp right out of the water. Wish I had some now. That was good, man, that was sure good."

Eunice's mouth watered at the thought. "Your father was an alcoholic?"

"Yeah. Well, he left my mother. He left us when we were kids. Ma had a hard life."

"I would imagine you did too then." She thought of her own life, secure, youngest of seven children, father and mother who cared so deeply about each other and for the family. "My mother had a hard life too, in a different sort of way. We had a large family—seven of us. My oldest sister had the flu and pneumonia in World War I and developed encephalitis causing a lesion in the brain. She couldn't speak or coordinate very well. It was a hardship on the whole family. Mother handled her very well. Esther would get so frustrated, poor girl. Couldn't make herself understood sometimes. And then, many times, mother would have to leave all of us and take Esther by train seventy-five miles to Duluth where they'd stay for days, having Esther examined and tested." Eunice lapsed into thought. What a strong woman her mother was. All her life she was weaving the pattern that now characterized her in old age, Eunice thought. They had almost lost her mother once. Her father had gathered all the children around the bed and together they had asked God to spare her life, and he did.

Bill burst into the room. "We gotta get outa here! The landlord's been here. I don't think he's

49

suspicious yet but he's coming back in a little while."

They helped Eunice into her boots and coat. Swiftly, they guided her down a few steps. She stood and waited. It was daylight. Where would they put her this time? On the floor in the back?

Saturday, Gunnar

Early Saturday morning, Bruce and Oliver approached Gunnar. "We've got word that forty FBI men will be coming at daybreak to search for clues."

"Forty of them!"

"Yeah, thorough aren't they? Wonder what they'll find—if anything."

"I wonder. They should be here pretty soon then."

"The press conference will have to be postponed, they say, until ten o'clock."

At ten, Gunnar stood with his son John and Oliver and Bruce on the porch of his house. After quickly summing up Eunice's disappearance and the poor contact made with the kidnappers the day before, he said, "All I ask is the safe return of my wife. The FBI has promised not to interfere. We are awaiting further instructions. We will comply with demands and will follow instructions completely." Then he addressed his wife. "Eunice, I love you and all of us offer prayers for you."

When they got back in the house, Brady took

Gunnar aside. "When they call, you should be prepared to meet their demands at once."

"I intend to. I'll go myself, of course."

Brady met the level gaze of this strong man. "It has risks. We would recommend that you allow one of our men to take care of it. Danger is our business."

"But Clay, she's my wife. I'm willing to take the risk. I have no right to expect you or anyone else to endanger yourselves doing what I should do."

"It isn't only the risk, Gunnar. You have to consider that our men are trained to act swiftly under changing circumstances. They've been taught every possible action and reaction."

"Yes, I can understand that."

"Now Donovan—he's the same height as you and close to the same build. Put your windbreaker and cap on him—why, his glasses are even like yours. It seems to me he could double for you. Why don't you pray about it?"

Once more, Gunnar called John and Oliver and Bruce, and this time Jim Holm, into a bedroom. "Brady suggested we pray about the matter of the ransom drop when and if the kidnappers call again. We should be prepared. We should know exactly who's going to do it so whoever it is can proceed at once according to their demands. No, John, I don't think I would let you risk your life for me—or for Eunice. Naturally, I wanted to do it myself, and still find it hard to say I'm going to let someone else do this. She's mine. I'd risk my life for her. But the FBI are trained for this and are quite determined that they should do it for me—for us. Yet, we feel we should ask God for wisdom before we make a decision.''

Bruce and Oliver both prayed aloud, asking for guidance. They were also concerned that the witness for Christ should not be blurred through any action taken. Gunnar went from the room in absolute confidence. The FBI man would do it instead of him.

"You'll have to fill me in on some of the things about your life I might be expected to know," Donovan said as he sat with Gunnar, having coffee.

"Right. I will. Where to start?"

"Start by telling me about Eunice's background.''

"You mean, like where she grew up and went to school?"

"Yeah, even farther back. Were her folks from the old country?"

"Yeah. O.K. Her folks came from Finland, same as mine. Our parents were Swedes who settled across the border in Finland and were called 'Swede-Finns.' ''

"Yours and hers?"

"Yes. Her father was a carpenter. He came to America and got a job with a mining company in northern Minnesota. They were married before he left and they had two children. When he had enough money, he sent for them. He later formed a partnership with a Mr. Erickson. Her father did painting and interior decorating, and the partner did the carpentry. During the depression, the Chisholm school district hired

52

him as superintendent of buildings and maintenance."

"He was lucky."

"Yes, they had seven children. Many men were unemployed. Then too, he always had extra medical expenses."

"How's that?"

"Eunice's sister, the oldest girl, Esther, developed St. Vitus dance after the flu during the war. Eunice was taken care of a lot in those days by the second oldest girl, Elsie. She's also a nurse—lives in Florida. To this day, there's a special relationship between those two girls. Sort of a mother-daughter relationship. Did I tell you Eunice was the youngest?"

"Youngest of seven." Donovan was making notes.

"The brother Melvin was two years older than she, and her playmate. He also is special to Eunice although the whole family is very close."

"Big families are like that."

"Eunice went to school in Chisholm. Good school . . . supported by the mining companies. Had a swimming pool—"

"No kidding?"

"And band and orchestra. Instruments were on loan from the school. She was also very active in the church. When her parents settled down there, there was no Swedish church so they started one. An itinerant minister came once a month, and three Sundays a month I understand her father did lay preaching in Swedish."

"Quite a man!"

"Indeed! Eunice had an excellent relationship with her father. He was strong, even tempered, responsible—"

"Eunice works at Mounds-Midway School of Nursing?"

"Yes, she counsels students and teachers there. Also counsels faculty as they relate to students."

"Tell me a little about where she worked before you married her."

Gunnar and Dick Donovan sat together over many cups of coffee as Gunnar informed Donovan of some of the personal matters he should know in order to impersonate Gunnar. He told him about their recent trip, things about her family and his, her personality, jokes they shared, things they both liked to do, common concerns. "Dick, should you at any time find on this ransom run that you have to wait in a bar, you should know that my drink is never stronger than a tonic water with a squeeze of lime in it."

"You don't mean it."

"Yes, I do—a tonic water with a squeeze of lime in it."

Saturday, The Bergs

"Mother?" Ruth had been holding her mother's hand as Mrs. Peterson slept.

Waking now, Mrs. Peterson's white head lifted. "Ja?"

"Mother, we think we better stop at Gunnar's and see if they've heard anything from the kidnappers. Then we'll go on home."

"Ja. All right."

The FBI blockade a half mile from Eunice's home reminded them harshly of the reality of the kidnapping. As they approached the house, they saw strange men about the house and garage. "More FBI men, no doubt," Wally ventured.

Ruth introduced Clay Brady to her mother, then led her into the house. When she saw Gunnar, Mrs. Peterson fell into his arms. "What did our Eunice do to deserve dis?" Gunnar had no reply. They held each other, both of them weeping.

Pulling herself together, the old lady said, "Did you hear anyting more?"

"Not a thing."

"I don't believe God vill let anyting happen to Eunice. I belief he'll take care of her. Eunice is strong. She'll beat dose men. You vait and see."

Clay Brady stood with Ruth and Wally. "She's a real trouper. I admire your mother. I admire her faith. But I agree that she'll be much better off at your house, Mrs. Berg, where it's quiet."

"Did your men find anything when they were out looking for clues?" Ruth asked.

"Not a lot. They found some snow packed down out there in the trees, and some cigarette butts and empty wrappers. It could be where they'd been watching the house from."

When the Bergs arrived at their home in South

St. Paul, Brian, age fourteen, was glad they were back. "The phone's been ringing constantly. I finally just quit trying to tell everybody—I quit trying to answer questions and just said you'd call back. Look at this." It was a long list. "Besides this, a lot of them just said they wanted you to know they're praying for you and for Aunt Eunice—for all of us. I wrote their names down too."

Ruth looked at the list of those who had pledged to pray without asking anything in return. Tears filled her eyes as she thought of the marvelous privilege of being a member of the household of God. One family. One Father. One Elder Brother at the Father's right hand making intercession for them right now.

Mrs. Peterson, a rather heavy woman, lowered herself wearily into a rocker in the family room.

"I'll have coffee ready in a minute, Mother. That will perk you up a little bit."

"Ja, dat's all right." She shut her eyes but the pain she was feeling lay drawn across her lids.

Ruth's heart ached for her mother—that she had lived to see this day! How blessedly merciful it would have been if she had been spared this dreadful day! How much better to have died at an earlier age!

Eighteen-year-old Randy entered the room, breathless and excited. "You know what I think?"

Ruth looked up into his intense gray eyes and down at the tape recorder in his hand. "No, what?"

"I think the kidnappers are going to call here."

"*Here*?" Ruth asked. "No, why would they call here? No, I don't think so."

"Look," he argued, his brow puckered seriously, "our name's the only one that hasn't been in the news." He showed her the morning paper. "They think Astrid Fleming is Aunt Eunice's sister instead of Uncle Gunnar's, and your name hasn't even been mentioned in the papers. Whenever I hear about it over the radio or television I listen carefully and our name's never been on."

"Really? Well—"

"If I were the kidnappers, I'd try to make contact through some party that wasn't in the news and probably not being watched. Wouldn't you?"

"You've got a point there, Randy. Say, I'm proud of you."

"So, I think I'll just rig up the phone. I'll rig up the phone in the bedroom—" He headed for the bedroom, Brian at his heels.

Ruth followed, thinking it surely couldn't do any harm, and who knows? He might be right. In a few minutes he had hooked the tape recorder to the phone.

"There," he said with a firm nod of his blonde head, "if they call again we'll have their message on tape and there won't be any chance of misunderstanding it, see?"

"That was smart, Randy. It takes you to think of that." She still doubted that they would call her, but was thankful for Randy's interest.

57

Saturday,
Eunice

They were down in the garage. Bill said, "Now you aren't going to like this."

Eunice chilled through.

"—but we're going to have to put you in the trunk for a little while. It—"

"The trunk? Oh, no! No!" Eunice tried to pull away.

"It's not—"

"No, no, I'll die. I'll smother. Please. Please. I'll get carbon monoxided."

He pulled her forward. "It won't be for long. We just have to make a phone call. Be quiet for a minute, will ya? Just a half hour or so—"

"Please don't put me in the trunk. I'll lie down in—I'll scrunch up on the floor. I'll do anything you say. Please don't make me."

"You won't smother. I know that. I've made a hole in here so air can get in."

"Please—"

"I rode around in the trunk myself for a while and it's safe. Come on."

"Please take me out in a little while. Oh, please don't make me." Bill lifted her. She tore at some loose weather stripping. He struck her head on the lid of the trunk. "We'll stop in ten minutes and open it up." The door of the trunk came down with a thick thud.

"Oh, my God. Do you see me here? Jesus. Am I going to die in this trunk?" Her pulse hammered in her temples and her aching ear seemed about to burst.

58

The car moved into the street. Should she scream? Would anybody hear her? Perhaps in a few minutes she would no longer be able to. Dared she risk it? What did she have to lose now?

They were moving right along. "God, have you forgotten me?" None of her family knew where she was. She wondered how they were praying for her. How many could really get through to God? She tried to think of ten people who had ever told her of unique answers to their prayers, ten who were so close to God that he would share his mind with them. Ten who would sense her situation and press close to God for answers. She hadn't ever heard of many miracles.

In spite of her congested nose, she smelled tobacco smoke. They must be smoking. Though she had the usual nonsmoker's aversion to the odor, it was actually welcome now, for it proved that some air must be coming through. Perhaps it *was* safe in there. She shifted her body around the tire in that small trunk, thankful it was carpeted and that they had thrown her blanket in on top of her.

"Are you O.K. back there?"

"I—I guess so."

They seemed to be driving around in circles. Once they stopped for a few minutes and Eunice wondered if they were calling Gunnar. Then they drove again, starting off with a screech of tires. She assumed Bill was driving and at about 50 miles an hour. He was pretty nervous. Eunice remembered the guns. "Oh, God, don't let anything go wrong. Help them get the money quickly and let me go."

He shall preserve thy going out and thy coming in—

Saturday, Gunnar

The dining room table was continually laden with food. Neighbors brought in hot dishes. Gunnar picked up a piece of cheese and wandered into the breakfast room. Jim Holm, who had seldom mixed with the others about the house, was in his chair facing inward to a corner with his Bible open.

Gunnar sat down by the window. A sparrow pecked at the suet Eunice had hung from the birdhouse, then it searched among the few remaining sunflower seeds for smaller grains. It pecked, then lifted its head heavenward.

How many times he and Eunice had sat here watching the birds. Finches, snowbirds, cardinals, woodpeckers, nut hatches, creepers, junkos, sparrows, and starlings. Would they ever watch here together again? This was March—the birds would soon return North. Would Eunice greet their return?

Behold the fowls of the air: for they sow not, neither do they reap, nor gather into barns; yet your heavenly Father feedeth them. Are ye not much better than they?

In this room was the forty-cup coffee pot repeatedly being emptied and refilled. Now Gunnar took a cup of coffee. The telephone rang.

John had been answering it most of the time. Now Gunnar's second son Craig had arrived and was manning the phone.

"Kronholm residence." Everyone converged on the breakfast room, always hoping for word from the kidnappers. "No, I'm sorry there's been no more news about Eunice. I'm sorry but we have to keep this line open on orders of the FBI."

Clay Brady said, "Hang up."

Craig nodded to Brady. "I'm sorry, there's nothing more we can tell you. We have to keep this line open."

Clay said, "Hang up! Hang up!" There was sharp urgency in his voice.

"WHAT'S GOING ON THERE?" It was the angry voice of a woman, crackling through the wire.

"Hang up. Hang up. *Hang up!*"

Craig put the receiver down. "She's an old friend of Mom's from California. She just wouldn't hang up. I finally had to hang up on her. Sure hate to do that. If people would just understand."

As the day wore on toward evening, Gunnar began to observe a change in the FBI men. They tended to go aside for conferences more frequently and emerged with serious faces. Earlier they had walked and sat with the family, talking and injecting humor here and there in what seemed to be a masterful effort to keep up morale. Now they showed their concern.

Gunnar became depressed. If the FBI were losing hope, how could he stand up? He walked the length of the house, back and forth, only occasionally noticing his fatigue. He hadn't eaten much for two days, and he had no appetite now. Anxiety pressed in on him. Did they know something they weren't telling? No, that wouldn't be like Brady and Harvey. They would tell him. But what if they weren't positive? Then they would wait. Did they fear she was dead? Oh, if only they might hear. If only the telephone would ring and it would be Eunice.

He sat down again in the family room. He imagined a car driving up and Eunice getting out of it. But it wouldn't happen that way. They might get a call from the police: "We have your wife." And then what? "She's in bad shape"? Or would it be, "She's in good shape, not too much worse for the experience." Or would they say, "We *found* your wife—" He buried his head in his hands. "God, do you see me here? Are you still with me? Don't you know how hard it is, not hearing anything? Not knowing? Do we have to go through another night like this?" It seemed God didn't hear.

Despair and hope, bitterness and trust vied for supremacy. He couldn't pray anymore. He was numb.

Saturday, Eunice

Eunice looked at her watch, holding it up to a crack of light near her face. 6:15. She had been in that trunk since 3:00. They were shouting something. "What?"

"Can you give us some more numbers where we might reach your husband?"

"Yeah, let's see—he has a brother Oliver—"

"The one that lives across the lake?"

"Yes."

"No, we need other ones."

Eunice had thought often of her sister. In her fear and anxiety she had thanked God that it had been she and not Ruth who had been kidnapped. Poor Ruth, she would be beside herself during this ordeal. "Well, try 435-9000," she shouted.

"435-9000? We're writing it down. O.K. Do you have any nicknames?"

"Euny."

"Euny?"

"Yes!" She could hardly make them hear her.

A few minutes later, the car stopped again. "Oh, God. Make Ruth be at home. Help them get hold of Gunnar."

Saturday, The Bergs

"Keno" Peterson, Eunice's and Ruth's brother from Chisholm, Minnesota, had arrived and another brother, Melvin, was expected from Washington, D.C., at 7:30 in the evening.

"Melvin says he'd rather be here not knowing anything than there," Ruth explained to Mrs. Peterson.

"That's the way I felt," Keno said. "It's awful

63

not knowing. And Melvin's been calling every coupla hours."

"Every two hours or so. Randy?"

Randy came into the kitchen from the living room.

"Would you get Melvin from the airport? Dad and I want to go to church. They're having an all night prayer meeting for Euny and we'd sure like to go."

"Sure. I'll leave about seven. What time is it now?"

"Twenty minutes of." The phone rang.

"I've got it," Wally said, heading for the bedroom. Ruth and Randy followed. "It's for you, Ruth." He looked at her questioningly, waiting to see who it was.

Randy pressed the recording button.

Many people had been phoning. "Hello," Ruth said.

"Is this Ruth?"

It was not a familiar voice. She alerted her family with her eyes. "Yes, who is this?"

"A friend of Euny's." Ruth felt herself get warm. Only intimate friends and family called her that. This call seemed different. She nodded urgently at Wally.

"Can you get hold of Gunnar?"

"Yes, I think so." Her heart was pounding. Stay calm, she told herself. She sat down on the edge of the bed, squeezing her eyes shut, forcing herself to concentrate.

"Tell him to be at your house in thirty to forty-five minutes. We'll call back then. No police, no guns, nothing."

Ruth slowly and carefully repeated everything he said. She hung up. "It—was—*them*."
She was trembling violently. "We've got to get
Gunnar over here." She took a deep breath as
she dialed the Kronholm number.

Randy played the tape over the phone. There
was no mistaking that message.

Saturday,
Gunnar

Everyone moved into action. In the
garage, Dick Donovan crawled to the floor in the
back of Gunnar's Chrysler. They threw a blanket
over him and Gunnar drove to the Bergs.

The FBI had instructed the Bergs to clear out
their garage so that the Chrysler could move
directly into it. As they drove in, Ruth and
Randy appeared, in a great state of excitement,
at the door to the house.

"Hurry, Gunnar," Ruth called. "They're on
the phone again. They say they can't wait."

Both men rushed into the house through the
kitchen.

"The bedroom. It's in the bedroom," Ruth
whispered excitedly, leading the way. Wally
and Randy bumped into each other as they
jumped aside to make room in the hall.

His breath coming hard, Gunnar said, "Gunnar Kronholm speaking."

"Are the police with you?"

"No. How's my wife?"

"She's fine. She's scared but otherwise all

right. Follow instructions carefully and everything will be all right."

"I'll do everything you say." Gunnar was still panting. "But how do I know you have my wife? I've got to give you a test question so I know I'm dealing with the right party."

"Ask it and we'll give you the answer the next time we talk. Go to the phone booth on 66th Street, three blocks west of Lyndale in Minneapolis. Be there at eight o'clock and we'll give you further instructions."

Gunnar checked his watch. 7:20 now.

The man asked "What's the question?"

"The question—ask Eunice—ask my wife—what we did after the opera our last night in Rome."

"What you did—"

"After the opera our last night in Rome."

"—in Rome. O.K."

Swiftly, Donovan put on Gunnar's wristwatch, cap, and windbreaker. Since they had not been told how much money to bring, he brought what they had put together—$22,000.

As he got into Gunnar's car, Gunnar grasped his hand. "God keep you—"

Things were moving at last.

Saturday,
Eunice

They were on the road again. They were shouting at her. It sounded like Jerry.

"Your husband wants to know for sure that you're O.K."

"Tell him I'm O.K.," she answered, but her voice cracked. "I'm O.K."

"We did, but he wanted us to ask you a test question so he's sure you're all right."

Jerry's voice was strained. He must be turning toward the rear to yell at her.

"What is it? What's the test question?"

"What did you do special the last night in Rome?"

"We went to the opera," she yelled back.

"Something else, he said, besides that."

Was that really the same person—was she, the woman in the trunk of this car, the Eunice Kronholm who had gone to the opera in Rome a week ago with Gunnar and afterward—

"We went out for pizza."

"Pizza, that must be it."

So they were negotiating with Gunnar. He knew she was still alive. It wouldn't be much longer. Maybe the next time they stopped they would let her go. A sleepy sense of calm crept over her. Eunice slept.

The need to use a bathroom woke her. If their situation required that she travel in the trunk of the car, she feared they would not let her out to go to the toilet. They continued to drive. They had talked of Chicago, but why would they take her there if Gunnar were right now getting the money for them? *Maybe they weren't really planning to let her go!*

"Are you all right back there?"

"I need to get to a bathroom soon. Will we be getting there pretty quick?"

"It won't be too much longer."

Eunice could hear them talking to each other but couldn't understand what they were saying.

She was becoming very cold. "Dear God, please make everything happen quick for my release. Help Gunnar get the money and please keep these men from getting too nervous. We've got to stop driving pretty soon. I don't know how much longer I can —"

There was just room for her to lie on her right side as she shaped herself around the spare tire. She could lean toward her back to take some pressure off her hip from time to time. Cold as she was, she realized that God had provided for her before she could know how to provide for herself. How thankful she was that yesterday morning, as she had prepared to go to the beauty shop, she had dressed warmly, including, at the last minute, her leather coat "to keep out the wind," she had thought. Ordinarily, she wore boots only after a fresh snow fall, but this time she wore them to keep warm, because of having been ill. With her on this entire experience was her long acrilan scarf and her very own blanket. She took it as her earnest from God that he would take care of her.

Right now her feet seemed made of ice, even in the boots.

They were shouting at her. "We're going to have to stop for gas. You have to be very quiet and not make a sound or you'll bungle the whole job. Your husband's getting the money together and whether you get out of here or not depends on how well you do what we say. So be quiet. It will make a noise coming in near you there, but don't you do or say a thing, understand?"

"O.K. I'll be quiet." Even as she promised she wondered what would happen if she would start to scream. She remembered the guns. One policeman had already been shot over this and she didn't want a gas station attendant to go next. She lay still, hardly breathing. She had become aware of a long thin object in a case lying next to the tire. Now she ran her fingers along the sides of it. It felt like a telescope. A shudder passed through her. How long had they watched her before they actually kidnapped her!

She became obsessed with the need to go to the toilet. There were bathrooms here. But she had to stay put. When would it end?

They started driving again. Eunice had no idea whether the gas station had been in the Twin Cities, or in Wisconsin, or South Dakota. They stopped twice about a half hour apart. Were they talking to Gunnar?

Oh, what could she do about her feet? By pushing the toes of one foot against the heel of the other, and by reaching as far down as she could with her hand, she managed to wiggle one foot out of its boot. She brought the foot up and clutched it with her warm hand. She rubbed and rubbed her icy foot. How blessedly warm her hand felt. How could she ever get her boot back on? She couldn't. She had done a foolish thing. Oh, when would they ever let her out? The boot kept dropping and tipping over. With her foot she edged it over higher and higher. Finally, she was able to grasp it with her hand. At last she eased her foot into it. It soon was as cold as it had been before. Both her feet would surely freeze.

They drove and drove. Eunice tried to figure out a way she could use as a bedpan the large boots stored in the trunk with her. If she should wet her clothing she would get very cold. She shivered uncontrollably as it was. Her ear ached. She had never experienced such discomfort.

They had stopped! Maybe they would take her out. She didn't dare call to them now. They stayed there for about ten minutes. Then they took to the road again. Eunice called, "I thought you were going to take me out back there. I can't stand it much longer. I'm just freezing and I can't wait to go to the bathroom."

"Just a little longer. In a little while, we'll take you out."

A few minutes later they were slowing down. "We're going to take you out now. You can't make a sound. There's no garage here. You have to get out of the car and in the door as fast as you can." They stopped, and she heard a car door. Then it was quiet.

Minutes passed. Had they deserted her? With immeasureable relief, she heard the key in the trunk lock. The door flew open. They half dragged—half lifted her out and set her on her feet. She sank. They held her and guided her soundlessly to a door. She stumbled into a room. They took her immediately to the bathroom. Eunice had to hold onto the sink and the toilet. There was barely room to turn around. She trembled from weakness and shook from the cold.

As she opened the bathroom door, a hand reached for her and settled her onto a chair. Jerry handed her a cup of water. She held onto it with both hands but spilled it getting it to her mouth. Complete exhaustion came over her. She couldn't hold herself up on that chair. "Could I lie down?"

Both men helped her onto a small bed. The mattress had dips and lumps but Eunice had never lain in a bed that offered her more comfort. They covered her up.

"What time is it?"

"11:15."

Almost at once, she fell asleep.

Sunday,
March 17,
The Bergs

Donovan slipped quietly in the side door of the Berg residence. Gunnar, who had been waiting in the living room, heard him. It was after midnight.

He hurried to meet Donovan. "How did it—?"

"They called it off."

"They called it off! Why? What went wrong?"

"They were very suspicious. Well, you remember I was to go to 66th and Lyndale. That was a drive-up phone at a filling station. I didn't get there right at eight o'clock. I was ten minutes late.

"The phone rang and I identified myself as Gunnar Kronholm. They had the answer to the test question and the man also knew that Mrs. Kronholm trained nurses, so it seems they're the right party all right."

"Did they say when—"

"In that conversation, they didn't mention the ransom or when they'd release your wife. The man I talked to warned me about contacts with law enforcement authorities and asked me if I had any electronic devices on me. I said I didn't, but he was suspicious. He told me to go to the Hub Shopping Center. There was a booth located under the sign that said, "Hub," and it was at 66th and Nicollet. He said it'd take me six to eight minutes to get there. When I got there I was to take off my coat, open my jacket, or sweater—whatever I had on—and pull up my shirt to make sure I had no recording devices on me."

Gunnar's face registered horror. "No! You were in great danger!"

"Well, I did as they said."

"Did you see anybody?"

"No, but I imagine they saw me."

Gunnar was still shaking his head.

"I had torn it off in a hurry, I'll tell you!" Donovan lifted his shirt and Gunnar saw the tape marks.

"Were you able to convince them?" Gunnar asked.

"I rather think so. They said I should be back at the same place at 6:30 this evening."

"After you tore off the electronic stuff, how did you—?"

"All I had left was the telephone."

"I see."

"They said they wanted $400,000 and they told me exactly what denominations they wanted it in. But I told 'em two was all we could get. They said, 'Well, then, get it from the bank,' and I said the bank doesn't have that much money in the denominations they wanted. I said I could never get $400,000; I convinced 'em two was the top I could do. I'm to have it with me tonight. Well, I better get over to your house."

"Ruth's getting you some breakfast. Bet you're beat."

73

"Thanks, Mrs. Berg, but I don't think I'll wait to eat. I'll sleep a while."

Another day without Eunice. Dick had already been forced to endanger himself. How might it end?

Sunday, Eunice

It was still dark when they woke Eunice. "We've gotta move." Bill handed her her boots. Jerry helped her into her coat.

Fear seized Eunice again. Back in the trunk? No, thank God, the door was open for her. "Lay down in the back. Nobody'll see you."

An hour or so later, Bill spoke gruffly. "Now you two change places."

They hesitated momentarily. "Listen here, I said change places!" Jerry tumbled into the back seat tangling with Eunice as she scrambled into the front.

"Now when I stop," Bill said, "you slide over into my place and out my door, understand?"

They went directly into what seemed like a motel.

"You can lay down on this bed," Bill said.

It was a large double bed with a firm mattress. "Would you mind if I crawled into it?"

"No, go ahead." He seemed more relaxed. "There's a lake out here. Do you want to go fishing?"

"Not right now, Bill. I'm sleepy." This light banter helped to dispel some of her fear. She began to relax. The need to sleep again over-came her.

She awoke to a radio. "We've got a radio here. Would you like to listen to it?" Jerry asked.

"I sure would."

"Anything special? I don't know the stations around here."

"Well, try CCO—that's 83." Eunice hoped to get some news about the ransom money.

"Is this it? No? You better try yourself."

Eunice got up and felt her way toward him. He put out his hand to her. Bending down, she turned the dial. Suddenly, she heard organ play-ing, then a familiar voice. "Oh," she exclaimed, "I know this one. This is KTIS. It's almost church time. Do you mind if I listen to church?"

"No, go right ahead."

"We take you now to the First Baptist Church, in downtown Minneapolis—"

Eunice recognized the familiar voices heard regularly over the air from that stronghold of evangelical Christianity. This morning they were dedicating infants.

When the last baby had been blessed, the congregation joined in singing the doxology. It seemed incredible to Eunice that churches all over the country were worshiping as usual this morning as she remained a captive. How often she had sung it. Now here she was, one poor shaking creature "here below" in the hands of men who didn't know God.

The choir had burst into the anthem:

Praise to the Lord, the Almighty, the King of
    Creation.

O my soul, praise him, for he is thy health
and salvation.

Eunice prickled with feeling. How many
times she had sung that song in church. She
strained to catch every word:

All ye who hear,
now to his temple draw near.

She worshiped.

Praise to the Lord, Who o'er all things so
wondrously reigneth.
Shelters thee under his wings, yea so gently
sustaineth.
Hast thou not seen how thy desires e'er
have been
Granted in what he ordaineth?

Yes. Yes, she had seen how her desires had
been granted in what God had ordained for her
in the past. Had he ordained this kidnapping?
She still wrestled with that. She desired a per-
fected faith. Would God work through this experience to grant her that? Would he prove himself to her in a way she had never known before?

Ponder anew what the Almighty can do
If with his love he befriend thee.

Eunice began to see herself off to the side as in
her spiritual vision she imagined what God
might do.

Praise to the Lord, O let all that is in me
adore him!

All that hath life and breath, come now with
    praises before him.
Let the Amen sound from his people again.
Gladly for aye we adore him.

Eunice whispered, "Amen, Lord. Let it be according to your will."
The anthem was over, it was the congregation's turn to sing:

Children of the Heavenly Father,
Safely in his bosom gather.

In her imagination, Eunice was swept to a little Swedish church with her three brothers and three sisters all sitting between her parents. Mentally, she sang along in the Swedish:

stjärnan ej på himlafästet
Fågeln ej i kända nästet.

The choir sang:

God his own doth tend and nourish.
In his holy courts they flourish.
From all evil things he spares them;
In his mighty arms he bears them.
Neither life nor death shall ever
From the Lord his children sever.

Again Eunice remembered her father. On his deathbed, he had summoned her. "How much vud it cost to keep Esther in a nursing home?" he had asked. "I haf alvays hoped she vud never haf to go to vun. I haf so much prayed that God vud take her first. I haf safed some money—"
Eunice had urged him not to worry about

Esther. "Dad, there are still six of us besides mother. Esther is now our concern. We'll take care of her."

And they had. But Esther grieved for her father. Less than a year and a half later, Esther too had died, at the age of 51, having wasted away to less than fifty pounds.

The organ grew louder:

> Praise the Lord in joyful numbers;
> Your protector never slumbers.
> At the will of your Defender
> Every foeman must surrender.

Softer now:

> Though he giveth or he taketh,
> God his children ne'er forsaketh.
> His the loving purpose solely
> To preserve them pure and holy.

Tears flowed down Eunice's cheeks. Holiness. That was what God wanted in her life. She prayed, "Lord, today every vestige of security I have is in you. My 'foemen' are getting pretty rattled at times and they have guns. One man has already been injured. Will it be life or death? I'm not afraid now, Lord. Even death will never sever me from your love. But Gunnar." A sob tore at her chest. "Oh, Father! He would be so alone again."

Someone was reading Psalm 103: "... and forget not all his benefits." Consciously, Eunice brought every thought under subjection. "Thank you, Father, that I have not been hurt. Thank you that I have all the water I want and

78

sometimes have food. Thank you that these men are not cruel to me." For a moment she felt this was what Gunnar was praying for her—that she would not be tortured or molested. "And Lord, I'm so glad I didn't have Knop with me Friday morning when I was taken." She was certain her precious little Yorkshire terrier would have been disposed of by this time. "Thank you for the opportunities I've had to witness to these men and that even now Jerry is listening to this service with me. Cause it to touch his heart."

"As a father pitieth his children, so the Lord pitieth them that fear him."

Eunice wondered what father images this evoked for Jerry.

Her father blended now in her mind with her heavenly Father. For a moment they were one and the same, comforting her, laying a hand across her brow. She remembered how strong she had considered her father to be and how protected she felt as a child. They used to go in a boat, many of them at one time. Eunice smiled slightly now as she recalled a neighbor once saying, "If there'd be a storm and the boat would capsize, all those children would jump on Peterson's back and expect him to bring them to shore."

Her father had been a gentle man. If his children resisted doing their work, he would ask them to do it, and if they hesitated further he would say, "Shall I do it? Do you vant me to go?" Then, shamed, they would perform their tasks.

The offertory was a piano solo. Eunice fitted the words to the music:

> Be not dismayed what e'er betide;
> God will take care of you.
> Beneath his wings of love abide;
> God will take care of you.

It seemed this entire service had been planned for her. She knew Bill Malam, the pastor of this church. They had both worked at Bethel College when he was in the seminary.

> No matter what may be the test,
> God will take care of you.

God was showing in a tender meditative way he understood and would take care of her at the point of her greatest need. Tears coursed down her cheeks.

Bill Malam was praying now: "For some of us our human circumstances are most difficult, but Christ is here to help. We pray for those in deep waters. We ask that you give them courage and hope. As we are here, or as we have gathered by a radio, we acknowledge we need strength. As we move through life, we pray that from us may flow rivers of living water that will make people hunger and thirst for righteousness. Regardless of what turn of events might take place, we know you have a plan, and we are part of that plan."

It was as though he were thinking especially of her. A woman was singing: If we could see beyond today as God can see.

Oh, how Eunice wished she could know how

this would turn out. As though her mind had been read, the woman sang:

> If we could see—if we could know—we often say;
> But God in love a veil doth throw across our way.
> We cannot see what lies before
> And so we cling to him the more.
> He leads us 'til this life is o'er.

God hadn't left her. She was very much in his care. She would cling to him the more.

Rev. Malam preached on "The Fatherhood of God." He said, "Even the hairs of your head have a value. God loves the world, but there is joy in heaven over one sinner that repents. He loves you individually. All believers are a part of his family. He is 'our' father."

One day, Eunice had disobeyed her father. She was in 8th grade and had refused to play her violin, which she despised. Seldom provoked to anger, her father now warned that unless she obeyed him, she would not be allowed to accompany her parents in the summer when they went to the annual church convention. That being months away, Eunice felt he would forget and she still refused to practice.

But he didn't forget. When that day arrived, Mr. Peterson announced that Eunice could not go. "Do you remember when you wouldn't play your violin?" No amount of pleading could make him change his mind. Eunice remembered that her mother had wept as she left her Euny behind. She knew now too that it had pained her father to so drastically keep his word. Yet, what strength she had sensed in him; now she took strength from it for this hour.

Bill Malam was finishing his sermon. "All believers are a part of his family. He is 'our' father. We trust that you are aware that your heavenly Father is watching over you this day."

Then the benediction: "May the grace of the Lord Jesus Christ and the love of God the Father and the fellowship of the Holy Spirit be with each of you now and forever. Amen."

Jerry had listened to the entire service with her. He gave no sign of what he was thinking.

"Did you listen now?" Eunice asked.

"Yes," he answered simply.

Soft music filled the room. Then Eunice said, "Jerry? Jerry, how's that policeman that was shot Friday night?"

"What policeman? I never heard anything about that."

"Bill said a policeman had been shot. Bill thought one of your men got nervous when he was stopped or something."

"Never heard a thing about it. I have an idea Bill just—well, I'll have to find out. I think he just said that to keep you nervous."

The music stopped and the radio announcer came on with "We at KTIS wish to encourage our listeners to pray for the safe return of Eunice Kronholm to her family. Mrs. Kronholm was abducted from her home Friday morning."

"Did you hear that?" Eunice's face relaxed in a big grin. "That means that thousands of people are praying for me. Isn't that something?"

"I can't believe it." Jerry repeated, "I can't believe it."

Soon after that, Billy Graham and the "Hour of Decision" came on. Jerry and Eunice listened as the gospel was forcefully given.

"When I get out of here—when I get my share of the money, I'm going to give a lot of it to good causes," Jerry solemnly declared.

"Good," Eunice commended him. "Which ones do you have in mind?"

"Well, I don't know yet."

"Well, I might know a few. Billy Graham for one. You just heard him."

"Yeah, he's a pretty good speaker."

Bill, who had been gone all day, returned. He had food. Eunice smelled meat. Quarter-pounders they were! From MacDonald's. And milk. Nothing had ever tasted so good before. She wondered where they had gotten the money now when they had been so penniless.

"Bill," Eunice said, "we heard over the radio early this afternoon that thousands of people are praying for me."

"Oh, yeah?" Bill chuckled slightly. "They're prayin' for the wrong one." Then seriously he said, "I wantcha to be thinking about what you can write in a note to your husband. You can say anything you want, and then I'll tell you what to write."

When she had finished eating, Bill said, "Now I wantcha to write that note. No, don't take off your blindfold. You can push it up enough to look down on the desk. Here's a piece of paper and a pen."

Eunice reached for her purse. "I have my own pen. If I use my own Gunnar will recognize it."

"First, I want you to tell him in your own words what your condition is. He wants to know. Then I'll tell you what to write."

Love welled in Eunice's heart at the thought that Gunnar's anxiety over her would be partly alleviated. "Dearest Gunnar, please, honey, hurry. Try and cooperate in every way. Everyone is so nervous."

"Tell 'im no FBI—no electrical equipment," Bill said.

Eunice wrote: "They say 'no FBI men, no electrical equipment.' I'm fine, just very weak and weary. They have been very good to me, so don't worry, please. God is good and you are so good. I love you so much and will be able to come home if everything is carried out. If there is any device in the carrying case or car, please remove it now. It won't help. I'm sure you know. Hoping to see you soon. All my love, Eunice."

Then Bill gave her a sheet of instructions. "Copy these."

Eunice tried to memorize what she wrote but found it too involved. Gunnar was being sent all over—mostly night spots in Minneapolis and suburbs. "I hope you'll give him lots of time. I'm sure he doesn't know where these places are."

"We'll give him enough. He'll find 'em."

Bill grabbed the note. "I'm going to see that he gets this now. If everything turns out, you should be on your way home." He read the note in a whisper. "No, no, this isn't right. It's supposed to be 'Wait inside *twenty* minutes,' change this here. And make this 'west end of parking lot.' It's plain enough to copy." He seemed angry and jittery. "Now you aren't going to like this."

He stood silent for a moment as though deliberating a course of action. Eunice felt herself get hot. What were they going to do? The last time he had said that, they had put her in the trunk.

Bill continued, "But we're going to have to tie you up for a while."

"Tie me up! What do you mean?" While he spoke Eunice felt a heavy rope brush her wrist.

"Well, we both have to go for a while now." He took her hands. "We can't leave you here alone untied or you'll leave."

"I won't leave. Really, I'll just stay right here." She pulled her hands away. "Please don't tie me up."

"I believe you would stay here, but if those other guys came and found we hadn't tied you up it wouldn't look too good for us. We'll tie your hands and feet and you can wait on the bed. It will only be half an hour or so."

They tied her hands together back to back. Then with the same rope they tied her feet together. There she lay in a fetal position on the bed. "If someone comes to the door just say you're in bed." They left.

Eunice had no idea where she was or what worse evils might befall her if they should return and find her trying to escape. She decided if the ransom was about to be paid her best bet would be to ride it out their way.

Time dragged. She couldn't change her position because of the way she was tied. But she was glad they hadn't gagged her and was thankful to be lying on a bed. And at least she was warm.

Sunday, The Bergs

Sunday at the Bergs found a few extras at the dinner table: Mrs. Peterson and her sons Keno and Melvin, two members of the FBI, Gunnar and Greg, a friend of Randy. Not wanting to miss any of the action after the kidnapper's call, Randy had delegated to Greg the job of bringing Melvin from the airport Saturday evening. Because Greg was at the house when the FBI took residence that night, he had been requested not to leave the premises. They wanted no one to be available to the media.

Since Donovan was taking Gunnar's place in the negotiations, it was of paramount importance that it not become known that Gunnar was at the Bergs. All drapes and shades were drawn. Every time the doorbell rang, Gunnar ran into a bedroom to avoid being seen.

As they ate, they conversed. "That doorbell early this morning sure gave me a start," said Gunnar.

"Me too, and twice. That was something," Ruth said.

"Joel came for my bag so he could deliver my papers," Brian explained, not for the first time.

"And then when he was through, he brought the bag back," answered Randy wryly.

"And scared us all half to death both times. Well, he had no idea, I'm sure, how he startled us each time."

The phones rang. With one accord they all started to rise. Donovan and Gunnar bolted for the bedroom where the telephone was rigged to the tape recorder. They soon returned. "It was Eric." Eunice's third brother from Hibbing, Minnesota, had telephoned many times, as had her sister Elsie Adams from St. Petersburg, Florida, and many nieces and nephews.

The afternoon passed. It was a day of nothingness. An FBI man monitored equipment set up in the dining room. Here Gunnar spent most of the afternoon. Keno restlessly paced. Grandma's head nodded a few times. They looked at the Sunday paper, watched television, answered the phone. Each time it rang, several of them collided in the narrow hallway to the bedroom. But no word came from Eunice, and no further word from the kidnappers.

Twice, well-meaning friends stopped by to comfort and visit the Bergs. Each time, Ruth and Wally had to keep them outside the front door. "I'm sorry, we can't invite you in today. We're waiting for word from Eunice or the abductors. Thank you so much for coming. I'm sorry; I hope you understand."

At 5:00 they again prepared Donovan for the ransom run. He now had the $200,000 bagged according to the instructions received the day before.

Gunnar had mixed feelings as he wished Donovan success in this second attempt. This man was more a friend to him than some he had known all his life. While Gunnar longed for an end to this matter and knew the demands had to be met before he could hope for Eunice's safe return, he realized Donovan was risking his life to do this.

Sunday,
Eunice

Over an hour later, Bill returned alone. "You didn't have your husband figured out very well." He untied her.

"What do you mean?"

"He's double-crossed us, I'm pretty sure." Bill paced about nervously.

Eunice's heart almost stopped beating. What in the world had gone wrong? "I can't believe that. I'm sure he would carry it out to the letter."

"Well, I don't know. Jerry's out there running around somewhere and there's cops all over the place." He swore. "We told 'im no cops and they're *all* over." She heard him lie down on the other bed.

He seemed at the end of his rope, in complete despair. What would happen to her if they fizzled the job? How could she calm him?

"My back's just killin' me," he complained. "I'm so tired I could care less what happens."

Eunice considered the plight of her captor. Truly the way of the transgressor is hard. If he didn't get some sleep he might do something rash. "Bill, would you like me to rub your back?"

"What?" Bill snickered. "You rub my back? So they break in here and see the abducted Mrs. Kronholm rubbing the back of a crook!"

"Well, if they come, I'll quick jump back in bed."

She felt her way to the other bed. "Let's see now, where are you?"

She felt soft material and followed it up to his head. Sitting down next to him on the bed, she rubbed his back, making a note of the fabric of his shirt. Not flannel, more like cotton and polyester.

Mentally she stood aside and viewed this incongruous scene. This man was her captor. He had stolen her with a gun, forced her into the trunk of a car for eight hours of driving without even a bathroom stop. She'd gone almost entirely without food for three days. She had no idea how it might end.

Bless them which persecute you. Do good to them which despitefully use you.

"Oh, that feels so good. Thanks. Gotta get up in a few hours to pick up—uh—Jerry."

She moved back to her bed and tried to find a comfortable position. There was no more sound from the other bed and Eunice supposed Bill must be in a deep sleep. She wondered if she should try to escape. But she had no idea where she was. By a lake? If they were in the country somewhere—no, she'd better stay. Surely the ransom would soon be paid and they would let her go.

Monday, March 18, Gunnar

Gunnar had sat up until midnight listening to the FBI receiving station for news of the ransom drop. Suddenly the announcement came over it that all radio communication would be stopped. This made Gunnar very nervous. What had gone wrong? Had Donovan been forced to expose his chest again and been hurt or killed? Perhaps he merely had to stop using the radio but was himself safe. Gunnar had tried to rest on the couch. No use. He paced the floor.

He heard the car pull into the garage. He raced for the side door. It was two o'clock.

Donovan looked cheerful. "You should have your wife back soon—if they keep their word."

"Thank God! What did they say?"

"They said they'll free her at daybreak."

"At daybreak! That's—"

"We better get back to your house fast. I'll tell you all about it on the way."

Donovan had driven the Chrysler into the Bergs' garage. Now he said, "I better drive. You lie down on the floor in the back this time." He covered Gunnar with the blanket which had covered Donovan Saturday night on the hurried trip to Bergs.

As they raced through the night stillness, Donovan related the events of his night: "You remember I was to go to a phone booth at 28th and Nicollet. Well, I was there in plenty of time and the call came through at 6:13. They told me to go to a booth at Portland and 78th Street. They said there I'd find a St. Paul directory and in its pages a note. I got there and picked up the directory and there it was. The note said to put the money in the trunk of the car and leave the key in the lock. They sent me all over town from one nightclub to another.

"Did anybody recognize you?"

"No, I'm pretty sure no one did. One of my co-workers was in one of those spots, I assume for the purpose of covering me—protecting me—but he didn't recognize me when I first came in."

"You had to wait in taverns?"

"Yeah. I'd have to go in and wait twenty minutes or so to give them a chance to take the money out of the trunk at any one of these places, but they never did. Reporters were following too close. I had my radio transmitter on again and was reporting to headquarters from time to time. The reporters were picking it up on short wave radio, I'm sure. Anyway, they were so close on my tail, and the abductors knew it, so they were afraid to surface. I had to quit using the radio.

"Well, after the last wait in a tavern, I went to the phone booth for final instructions. The money had still not been taken. They were pretty wary. When I talked to them this time I was able to convince them I had eliminated the media and wanted to complete the mission immediately. Actually, the FBI called the reporters off under threat of arrest for interference with the law."

"How late was it by this time?"

"A little before midnight. When I talked to them they said, 'There's a McDonald's Hamburger Stand on Highway 13 west of 35W, east of the first semaphore on Highway 13. Go there,' they said, 'and wait for a phone call.' At one o'clock it came. They said, 'Take the money from the trunk and put it in the front with you, in the right front seat. Drive south on 35W to the Burnsville Crosstown, and turn left by Embers. Take the frontage road to a turn-around by an old picnic area. Turn around, then stop and put the bag on the pavement beside the car.' I dropped it at 1:30."

"Did you see anybody?"

"Not a soul. But I'm sure they were there. Well, here we are." He pulled the Chrysler into Gunnar's garage. "Now to write my report and wait for daybreak."

For Gunnar, hope had revived.

Monday, Eunice

The alarm rang noisily, startling Eunice awake. "Wh-what?"

Bill shut it off. "I'll only be gone a little while. I won't tie you up if you promise not to scream or try to get away."

"I won't. I'll just stay here." She remembered the telescope in the trunk of the car. They were probably right now watching this house she was in. If this was a motel, there might be parties to the kidnap on both sides of her. She wondered for a moment if there was a phone in this room. She had never heard it used. What if she'd lift the receiver and "they" heard her, or were on the telephone? She didn't even dare to get up and peek out the window. The relationship she had worked hard to build with Jerry and Bill would be gone if they should catch her trying to escape. Surely she would be home with Gunnar soon now. She prayed herself back to sleep.

She woke when Bill returned. "The whole thing's gone to pot. We blew the whole thing." He dropped noisily onto the other bed.

Eunice's heart sank.

Bill said, "I'll tell you what, Jerry and I— if nothing else—we'll just drop you off at your house. You'll get home sometime this morning."

Her heart leaped with joy. But was he serious? She couldn't question him too much about the ransom money. She just lay there praying.

Then he said, "Well, I guess we better be going."

Eunice sprang to her feet.

"Oh, not too fast," Bill said. "We've gotta clean up here a bit first." She heard him wadding up paper and moving about as though cleaning up every speck of evidence.

It was still dark when he ushered her out the door to the car. "Go in the driver's side and slide to the other side fast. If I say so, take off your blindfold in a hurry. When I tell you to, put your head on my lap."

Eunice could hardly hold back her excitement. She was on her way home! The day was young. No matter where they might drop her, it was early enough for her to get home before dark.

About a half hour later, Bill stopped the car. She heard a familiar sound. The metal door of the garage where she had been on Friday. Could it be? Surely not—but yes, he was taking her up the stairs to the same room. Looking down, she saw the white shag rug. She sank to the floor in despair.

Monday, Gunnar

The family gathered at the Kronholm residence had listened with mounting excitement to the details of the ransom run as given over the FBI receiving station in the master bedroom. The term "package" had been given to the car and person who were to make the drop. Overhead aircraft surveillance vehicles were named "Eagle" and "Buzzard." At midnight, the word suddenly came that all radio communications would be stopped and any further communication would be made by telephone. They sat stunned. The drop had not yet been made and it became doubtful it could be made. Brady and Harvey told the family they might as well go to bed.

A few hours later, the news came to the FBI men that the drop had been made and the kidnappers would make contact in the morning, giving instructions as to Eunice's location.

When Gunnar and Donovan had returned, the women of the household persuaded Gunnar to try to get some sleep before daybreak when they would start waiting for word from Eunice. He consented to a mild sedative and slept for two hours on the couch in the living room, the first he had slept since Thursday night.

At nine o'clock, the FBI men in the house received the information that a local newspaper and a television station both possessed, and would publish around noon, specific details of the ransom drop. While Donovan had been out on the run, the FBI had ordered the media off the route. Yet now they were about to publish the names and places where Donovan, who was still believed to have been Gunnar, had made contact with the kidnappers.

"The kidnappers are very nervous," Donovan said. "Did I tell you that at one time they asked me where the FBI man was that I had in the back of my car?"

"What did you say?" Gunnar asked.

"I told him I didn't have an FBI man in my car, and then he said, 'Aw, come on, we know there are FBI men all over the place.' And the way they made me expose my chest on Saturday, and called off the first attempt—they're nervous all right."

Gunnar feared for Eunice.

Brady spoke. "We were told she would be

released today, this morning, if we complied with all their demands. Here it's eleven o'clock and still no word from either her or them." Looking steadily at Gunnar he said, "We have a man under surveillance."

Gunnar's eyes opened wide in surprise.

Brady continued. "We think he's in on the kidnapping and we're concerned that he's a dangerous fellow, judging by some of his actions. He seems to be planning to make a get-away—"

"Shouldn't you pick him up?"

"We were hoping he'd let your wife go first. But our men know that he has cleaned out the trunk of his car and put a suitcase in it. And he's changed clothes." Slowly and emphatically he said to Gunnar, "You have another decision to make, and this may be the most serious one of them all."

"Eunice's life is in danger, isn't it?"

"We feel it is. We can't anticipate how this fellow or these fellows will react when that ransom run is published in the paper at noon or on television. They might get desperate."

"What do you think we should do?"

"It's not the usual thing—to apprehend a kidnapper before he releases the victim. We think, though, that Eunice's future would be more secure if this man were picked up prior to the news release."

Gunnar nodding slowly said, "I see what you mean. I see the risks—either way."

Once more, the family went to prayer. This time, the circle included everyone. Gunnar told them the alternatives. They were desperate. Bruce and Oliver again led out in supplication. Gunnar, by nature coherent and controlled, cried out, "Dear God, save Eunice. Protect Eunice, Lord. We've done what was asked. Bring her back. Give her positive strength to combat and meet any needs she might have at this time. O God, we don't know what to do. Give us wisdom to make the decision what we should do." His voice dropped. "Look, God. See here. We're just human." He was sobbing. "We don't know the answers. We don't know what the next moment brings. All we can do as your children is cry out to you and here we are. Give us wisdom. Show us what to do."

The prayer session over, Gunnar told Clay, "Go out and apprehend the man." Having said it, he had absolute peace about it.

They continued to wait. And wait. And wait.

People were praying all over the house, sometimes aloud.

It was a time of tension and stress. Nerves frayed from excitement and lack of rest had worn thin.

Walking about the house, Gunnar talked briefly with first this one, then that one—his grown children, all here now except Sandra, whom the FBI had discouraged from coming, as she was about to have a child. John and Jan had been there since they had heard the news on Friday. Craig and Marcia had come on Saturday. Margaret and Linda had come from Philadelphia on Sunday. Mark, the youngest, had finally arrived Sunday night after learning of the kidnapping while on a Florida beach. Gunnar, even in his apprehension and fear, felt proud of every one of his children—of everyone in this house—for the way they were conducting themselves. No sharp word came from any one of them at any time.

How long would it be? Where was Eunice right now? Was she safe or— The possibilities of what might be happening to her right then shook Gunnar.

Tension was also mounting among the FBI agents. They spent much time in the one room which was strictly theirs, constantly in touch with their office. James Johnson had been picked up, but he refused to talk. He insisted over several hours of questioning that he knew nothing about the kidnapping. Eunice's car had been found in a lot at the Southdale shopping center. Edina police had pried open the trunk but had found no clue.

Gunnar learned that the FBI had ordered special equipment which could, from the air, detect *freshly overturned soil*. The thought sank into his consciousness. "They think—she's *dead*."

Every time the phone rang, the family converged on it to watch the expression on Craig's face as he answered. Never had time ground along so slowly.

Monday,
Eunice

Eunice was right where she had started on Friday. What had gone wrong? Bill was in no mood to talk. She'd have to ask Jerry. She was hungry. The last she had eaten was the hamburger about four o'clock the day before. "Do you have anything here that I might eat?"

"No," Bill said, "but we can make some coffee."

When the coffee arrived, it was in the hands of Jerry, whom Eunice hadn't seen since the night before when they had tied her up. "Jerry, Jerry, where were you?"

"I was out for five hours last night. Oh, was I cold! I've never been so cold in my life. Just can't get warm, it seems."

Eunice remembered the long ransom drop itinerary she had copied in her note to Gunnar. "I'm sorry you had to get so cold, Jerry. I feel pretty bad myself this morning. I thought everything was going well and that I'd be getting home this morning. Now I find—here—I—find we're right—where we started from." Eunice was sobbing.

Jerry came to her and knelt on the floor beside her. He put his arm around her shoulder. "You'll be home pretty soon. Don't worry."

"When? Do you know?"

"No, that's not up to me."

"Where will they let me go? Will I be tied up?"

"I'm sure you won't be in danger. If they tie you up, it won't be so tight that you can't get loose. Don't you worry no more. I want you to know we agreed there would be no violence."

Strange, yet not so strange. Her support was coming from one of those who had transgressed against her. "People do need people," she thought. How often she had said that in her classes. She felt truly comforted. Even so, she knew it would be Bill, not Jerry, who would decide her ultimate fate.

"Where's Bill now?"

"He left." Eunice knew that. Jerry either didn't know or wasn't telling where Bill had gone.

The day loomed before her. She had dealt with the problem of death and had given that up to God. She had felt his presence with her through everything she had gone through. But how much longer would this go on?

It occurred to her that she had to believe that God would answer a specific prayer. She had to believe he was that kind of God. She remembered the thousands praying for her, and believed Christians all over the nation were praying for her. They needed to believe he was a God who answered prayer. The whole world of the unsaved—they needed to be shown that God was a God who answered specific prayer. While she was thinking these thoughts the hour of "six o'clock" came to her. "God, I'm asking you to get me home by six o'clock tonight."

Goose bumps broke out over her body. She felt God had spoken to her "face to face." In the strength of this promise, she greeted the day.

She called to Jerry. He came, yawning loudly. She could imagine he was rubbing his eyes. "I fell asleep sitting on the register," he said. "Just couldn't get warm."

"I thought you'd left me. Would you take me to the bathroom?"

He took her hand. Eunice said, "I asked God to get me home by six o'clock tonight. Do you think I'll be home by six o'clock?"

"I sure hope so."

Eunice gave his arm a little squeeze of joy. When she came out of the bathroom, he handed her an ice cream bar. Eunice wondered where that had come from all at once. Suddenly suspicious, she decided to check her billfold. The six dollars she had were gone. The low-down criminals—stealing from her when she had done everything they'd said.

"You took my money!" She was scolding. "That really disappoints me. If you'd asked me for it, I'd've given it to you, but I don't like your just taking it."

"I didn't—take—it."

Eunice believed him, but she still felt betrayed. They were just criminals. In the end, they couldn't be expected to be anything else. She'd better not look to them for normal responses. So, she raged inwardly, it was she who had paid for the hamburgers and milk—yes and the ice cream bar.

Then it occurred to her—they had stolen her from her home, hadn't they? She'd been kept practically without food, had been forced into the trunk of a car where she was kept for eight hours without food or drink or bathroom privileges. Yet, here she was, indignant at them for taking her measly six bucks. She saw a gleam of humor in this. It was just that she had thought she had earned their trust, and now felt they deserved none from her.

A little radio had appeared as suddenly as the ice cream bar. Eunice occupied herself listening to Christian programs. Over and over, spoken words and gospel hymns bathed her spirit with assurance and comfort. At times, it was as though she were in a great concert hall listening to the "Hallelujah Chorus." God was so near.

Suddenly a news release came over the air: "Police have picked up a suspect who they think was involved in the Kronholm kidnapping case."

"Jerry, Jerry, did you hear that?" Her excitement brought Jerry fast. "Jerry, they picked up somebody. The radio says they picked up a suspect who they think was involved in the kidnapping. Do you suppose it was Bill?"

"I sure hope not!"

This news brought about a great change in Jerry. He became restless, pacing incessantly back and forth. Eunice switched the dial to WCCO in time to hear the announcement again. This time the name was given as James Johnson.

Jerry did not indicate whether it was Bill or not. He continued to pace, muttering occasionally to himself. "Why did I ever get into this mess?" A few minutes later, "How will I ever get out of it?" At one point he said, "Boy, if anybody mentions crime to me, I'm going to run the other way, man. No more crime for me. No, sir!"

Eunice lay quietly praying. Was God working out an answer to her prayer to be home by six o'clock? Jerry was speaking again. "I'm really

102

sorry we put you through all this. I didn't like it. I didn't like it at all. Don't worry. Nothing's going to happen to you."

Eunice marveled. Jerry and she had almost become friends. They wished each other well. It was as though they were in this thing together, both victims of a plot gone wrong.

Jerry was saying, "I couldn't start running right now, that's for sure. I should stay and get a good night's sleep first. Maybe try to borrow some money so I can get out of here."

It was 3:30 in the afternoon. Eunice said, "Jerry, I know the tellers don't close the windows at the bank until 5:30. Why don't you let me get you some money? Just a couple hundred—maybe five hundred dollars, or whatever you need. I'll try to get to my husband before the windows close. I'll put it in an envelope, Jerry, and we'll just put it wherever you want it."

"Oh, I have to think."

"I'll promise you it won't be marked money and in whatever denominations you want."

"I can't decide. I have to think about this for a while."

He went out of the room and paced the length of the house. She heard him—back and forth, back and forth.

He came back. Eunice said, "Well, Jerry, it's not going to do us any good to be here together."

"Oh, I'm pretty sure they're going to be coming around here pretty soon too, and I just don't know what to do."

"Well, why don't you let me go now?"

"I'd like to. I'd like to just walk away from this whole mess myself."

"Well, why don't you?" Eunice mentally stood aside and observed this scene: the victim giving counsel to the captor.

"Oh, I just don't know what to do. They've got me either way."

"Well, I think you should let me go right now." Eunice stood up quickly.

"Oh, there are workmen here. They're right next door."

Eunice had heard the pounding nearby.

Jerry said, "Wait—let's just wait about fifteen or twenty minutes and then we'll see."

Eunice sensed that Jerry was weakening. She began to feel she might get away soon. It was four o'clock. But what if by waiting they gave the police time to get there? Someone could get hurt. There might be a shootout. Or what if Bill came back—or the other men?

Eunice had no idea whether this James Johnson who had been arrested was Bill or one of the others supposedly involved. If Bill was in jail, one of the others, perhaps the one Bill had described as a sadist, would hurry to the apartment to finish the job with her. She became determined to quietly pressure Jerry until he'd let her go. God had given her the hour of six o'clock. That would be before dark and she would be able to orient herself somewhat.

"While we're waiting, Jerry, I think I'll put my coat and boots on."

"Yeah, well, I suppose you might as well."

Jerry walked to the window, "They're still

working around here." He paced back and forth. "I think we should wait until after dark. I think that would be much better."

Her heart sank. Too much could happen in the space of several hours. And how could she ever find where to go after dark? The wind gusted again. It sounded so cold. "Northwest winds gusting to twenty-eight miles per hour," the radio had said. She felt too weak to battle that wind and darkness too.

"Jerry, there wouldn't be any chance of getting you that money from the bank after dark. They close at 5:30."

"Oh, I couldn't get that money. You know, they'd nab me right away."

Eunice's greatest hope, her ace in the hole, disappeared. She seemed close to escape, yet far.

Then at quarter to five Jerry said, "Here's your blanket." He stood next to Eunice as they waited for the last workman to leave.

"Jerry, where can I go to use a phone?"

"There's an electrical place, a conduit. You might as well take off your blindfold. It doesn't make any difference anymore now."

Eunice carefully removed the taped mask from her eyes. She shook her head to focus her eyes and relieve the tight feeling around her temples. She avoided looking at Jerry. There would come a time when she would be asked to identify him, perhaps, and she felt he was the victim almost as much as she. She looked where Jerry was pointing.

"You turn left when you get to that electrical

conduit. Go to the first T and left. Then you'll run right into a shopping center. It's a good hike."

There was one car and one workman finishing up. As that workman left, something inside Eunice said, "Now." To Jerry she said, "Well, I think I'm going to go now."

Jerry said, "I think I'll go with you."

"Oh, Jerry, I think that would be a mistake. It would be less conspicuous if we left alone." He seemed to agree. She opened the door. Turning back, she looked at Jerry. He had a good head of dark hair and brown eyes. He wore dark-rimmed glasses. Their eyes met. She said, "Jerry, just remember this: I forgive you and God loves you." She hesitated for a moment then leaned over and kissed him lightly on the cheek. Turning, she stepped quickly outside, stiffening against the impact of the wind.

She walked as fast as she could. The wind whistled through her long scarf wrapped around her head. She put her hand up to protect her ear which ached already. Her purse in the other hand, she held up the blanket in front of her like a shield.

She looked furtively behind her. At a distance of about a half of a block, Jerry was following her. Had he changed his mind? She tried to run. She knew she couldn't make it up the hill. Exhaustion was about to overtake her. "O God," she prayed, "send a car. Send a car. Right away."

The next time she looked back there was a car! "Please make it stop. If it doesn't stop, I'm going to jump in front of it." It approached so fast that Eunice felt the driver wasn't planning to stop. She jumped in front of it and he stopped. The young man leaned over and rolled down his window.

"Please, could you take me to the Superette at the top of the hill? I understand there's one about a mile up the road."

"Sure, hop in. Having trouble with your car?"

"Ummm." Eunice looked straight ahead, aware of her disheveled appearance. She must not let him know she was the kidnap victim!

"Where is it?"

"Please, just take me to the Superette. I need to use a telephone. My husband will take care of it." She was almost crying.

She trusted no one. The youth had to leave the street and make a circle in order to drop her right in front of the door. She thanked him.

Hurrying into the small market, she asked the boy at the checkout counter, "Could I please use a telephone?"

"Sure." He guided her to the back.

As she started to dial her home number, she realized she didn't know the address of the store where she was. Leaving the phone, she went back to the front of the store. "I'm calling my husband to come and get me. Would you please tell me the address of this store? Where would he come?"

Eunice returned to the phone. She was shaking almost too much to do her own dialing, but she wanted no one to know she was the kidnap victim. They might refuse to become involved.

Monday,

Gunnar

The telephone rang. Again the house fell silent. Everyone moved toward the breakfast room.

"Kronholm residence—Craig speaking."

At the other end a whimper, then "Oh, Craig!"

He put up his hand to alert the family.

"Mom!"

"Oh, Craig, come and get me."

"We will, mom, we will. Where are you?—just a minute. Here's dad."

"Eunice! Oh, Eunice, Eunice."

"Come and get me, Gunnar, come and get me."

"I'll be right over." They were both crying too hard to talk. To be together again was the important thing.

He hung up and went for his coat and cap. The house exploded in laughter and crying.

"Where are you going?" Clay Brady asked.

"Well, I've got to get Eunice. Craig, did you get the number—the place—the address? Craig?"

"Yeah, here's the address. It's a Superette."

Clay spoke. "Look, the FBI will pick her up. You don't even know where that address is. They'll have her in a matter of minutes. Craig, call that store back and get her back on the phone. Don't let her get off. Tell her we'll have someone there to pick her up in a half hour or less."

Brady went to the master bedroom from which he telephoned the FBI office. Joseph Trimbach, the head of the Minneapolis department, was at his desk waiting. He said he would go personally.

Craig called the operator and asked for the number of the Tom Thumb Superette at 138th Street and Nicollet. He dialed the number. A mature male voice responded. Craig said, "A lady called from your store a few minutes ago—it may have been from a pay phone—I'm not sure. Would you by any chance—"

"Yeah, she's here. Do you wanna talk to her? She's shopping."

"She's *shopping!* Yes, would you please bring her—"

He heard the man calling to someone.

Monday,
Eunice

With her blanket and long scarf in the cart, Eunice had proceeded to go up and down the aisles. She hoped she looked like an ordinary customer.

"It's for you, ma'am." The store manager handed her the phone.

"The FBI are coming for you, Eunice. Hang on."

"Gunnar, do come and get me. You come, please, Gunnar. Hurry. They might come back. The men, any of them, might come in here and tell the store man I was theirs—that I'm drunk,

109

Gunnar, don't you see, or crazy. Gunnar, don't you see? You must take me away from here. Hurry. The store man won't know. He'd let them take me if they said I was just hysterical or something. Please, Gunnar."

"Eunice—Eunice dearest— Here's—"

"Mrs. Kronholm, your husband gave me the telephone. I'm Clay Brady with the FBI. I assure you, Mrs. Kronholm, that no one can get there faster than one of our men. Don't go with anyone who doesn't have the proper identification. Just stay right there and we'll keep talking to you. Here's your sister-in-law. She wants to tell you something."

Dorothy held Knop to the phone. He gave a little bark. "Knop's been missing you, Eunice. Do you hear him?" Eunice was in tears.

One after another, they all spoke a few words to Eunice. Gunnar had finally regained control of himself. He told Eunice it had been decided not to bring her to the house immediately as the press would give them no peace. Instead they had arranged for a doctor to meet them at the apartment of her friend, Joyce Johannessen.

"Oh," Eunice interrupted, "they're here now! Yes, they have identification. Yes, one is Joseph Trim—Trimbach. Oh, thank God!" She was trembling as she gratefully accepted his arm.

As they left the store, Eunice noted the hands of the clock. It was fifteen minutes to six. Tears of relief came into her eyes. God had come through.

Monday,
Gunnar

The wait was over. Eunice was leaving the store to join Gunnar at Joyce's house.

Gunnar went for his hat and coat a second time. He felt a hand on his arm. It was Clay Brady. He spoke to the entire family. "Look, we've prayed periodically these four days. God has been very present. He's answered our prayers. You wouldn't think of leaving the house now without pausing to thank him, would you?"

Every person in the house assembled in a circle—seventeen of them. Everyone wept. No one prayed in neatly formed sentences, but everyone prayed. All Gunnar could say was, "Thank you, God. Thank you, God. Thank you for bringing Eunice back."

Then they left. "It will take us about a half hour to get to Joyce's." Gunnar checked his watch. It was six o'clock.

They arrived there ahead of Eunice and her FBI escorts. "They'll be here any minute," Agent Harvey said. "When the car pulls up, just wait in here. We'll give you some time alone with her," he indicated a bedroom—"before we take a statement from her. Here they are now."

Gunnar recognized Joe Trimbach, as he helped Eunice from the car. Gunnar resisted a strong urge to run out there and seize her in his arms. Harvey opened the door for them and they entered.

Sobs already rising in his chest, Gunnar took

111

her arm and led her to the bedroom. Neither spoke. They held each other, both sobbing violently. They stood loudly weeping, then sat on the bed clutching each other, crying without words. They wept until they could cry no more, then still held each other, whispering each other's names.

"I was so afraid—I—would nev—ver see you"— his voice choked in his throat, "—see—you—a-gain." Gunnar finally managed to say.

He withdrew an arm's length to look at her better. She was flushed, one eye was bloodshot, her nose red. He pulled her back to him.

"Can't we go home?" Eunice asked wearily.

"Not just yet. The FBI want a statement from you when you're ready."

"I know. The man who released me is still out there. I called him Jerry. I don't believe he's a bad man."

"Not a bad man! Honey, they kidnapped you! How can you—Well, you can tell them all about it."

"I'm so tired. Oh, Gunnar, I'm so tired."

Again, he pulled her to him and kissed her eyes and head and neck. "Dick Burton's here. He'll have to examine you. Do you feel ready?"

She nodded and he went out, then returned with the doctor. After examining Eunice's heart and lungs and taking her temperature, he said he thought she should go to a hospital to have X-rays and an electrocardiogram. "The cornea of your eye seems irritated. You should have that checked too."

"I was blindfolded and it was pretty tight. I kept opening my eyes so I wouldn't go blind and the gauze irritated it."

"I see." He smiled. "Would you like something to eat?"

"Yes, I would."

To Joyce, Dr. Burton said, "Something light. Soup would be good. Something hot." He gave Eunice a tranquilizer.

After she had eaten, Mr. Trimbach said, "Now we'd like your statement. Just start at the beginning and talk into this tape recorder. Try not to leave anything out."

Somewhat refreshed now and becoming more relaxed, Eunice told the story. Occasionally, she would backtrack a little. Sometimes the agents asked questions. After an hour and a half she was totally exhausted. Every cell in her body yearned for a good night's sleep.

They took her and Gunnar to Mounds Park Hospital with FBI escort. But Eunice still could not go to bed. First there must be a thorough physical, complete with X-rays and cardiogram.

At midnight, she wouldn't have needed the sedative and sleeping pill but accepted it. They gave Gunnar one too.

They both dropped off to sleep within minutes. Two FBI men stood guard, one by their door and one downstairs.

Once during the night Eunice woke up crying. "Darling, you're safe now." Gunnar reassured her and she went back to sleep in his arms.

Wednesday, March 20, Eunice

No longer able to delay a press conference, Bruce and Oliver made arrangements for Eunice to hold it at Bethel Seminary in Arden Hills.

The day before had been spent in the hospital. In the morning, after Eunice and Gunnar had had a huge breakfast of grapefruit, pancakes, bacon, eggs, and coffee, Gunnar's children had come to see them. Their strong emotion had surprised Eunice. "They didn't expect to see me alive again," she thought.

In the afternoon, all the Petersons had come. When Mrs. Peterson came into the room, on Melvin's arm, and leaning on her cane, both Eunice and her mother broke down completely. They clung to each other. Neither of them could talk.

Everyone in the room was crying. Finally Mrs. Peterson said, "Tank God ve see you again. I knew God vudn't let you get hurt," but her sobbing belied her words.

Eunice and Gunnar had come to Bethel Seminary directly from the hospital. Now as they approached the microphones, Eunice's legs trembled. Family members had suggested she prepare her speech, but she had replied, "God took me through three and a half days of this and he's not going to leave me now."

She had to admit, she hadn't expected it to be quite such an event. Dozens of reporters stood about, their curious anticipation clearly evident. The U. S. Assistant Attorney, Thor Anderson, had telephoned to warn her not to say anything that would impede the apprehension and trials of the kidnappers.

Someone pinned a corsage on her. Others were pinning nametags on all the members of the family. Gunnar was answering a reporter. "Why do we have our family here? Well, they support us, and you know when you have six children, why it's great. We've got wonderful support."

Momentarily, Eunice thought of Sandy, still waiting in Appleton, Wisconsin, for her baby.

Bruce Fleming had said Dr. Gordon Johnson, dean of the seminary, would lead in an invocation. Eunice wondered how many press conferences opened with prayer.

Now Gunnar was speaking. "We're just delighted the way things have happened, that she's back with us and she's just been noble in this whole thing." He seemed nervous. "Sorry we had to delay the press conference because of Eunice's condition when she was taken. She was suffering from the flu and still had some effects . . ."

Like her aching ear. Eunice put her hand up to it.

Gunnar's nervousness seemed over. "I'd like

to say thanks to the FBI." Eunice wished he would just handle the whole thing. "Their understanding, their performance during this ordeal has been just outstanding; their primary concern at all times has been for the safety and ultimate return of Eunice unharmed, and also for the security of all the individuals involved.

"Thank you, too, to the neighbors who gathered around us and for the many friends and to the millions of prayer warriors that we had across the nation."

Eunice thought of the flood of telegrams and offers for help which had reached Gunnar. Letters were still pouring in, according to Craig and Marcia, who were staying at the house.

". . . it's been the thing that has held us up. Thank you very much, gentlemen."

It was her turn. All those reporters. Bruce gave one of them the nod to speak first.

"Could you please very briefly tell us how you were abducted and proceed through the kidnapping, including the time you finally escaped?"

As coherently as she could, Eunice told the episode from beginning to end. When she didn't know what to tell next, she asked for another question.

"How did you finally escape? What were the details of your getting away?"

"Well . . . we were moved from place to place. I had no idea where we were, if we were even in the city. There were two of them that were with me alternately. They were listening to the radios and getting progressively more nervous. You could hear them prancing back and forth and things like that. They said as soon as they got the money they would let me go. So my constant hope was that in a few hours I'd be let go as soon as they got the money.

"Perhaps the hardest was the tension of not knowing when I'd be released because every time I was going to be released something else happened.

"They kept saying, 'Well, we blew the whole thing and now we have to start over again.' So the tension was building within myself." The re-living of the story was making her tense now.

"At the end, I was left with one of the abductors and he had heard one of the men had been taken and at that point I tried to talk him . . . after a couple of hours I succeeded, by the grace of God, in getting him to let me go."

"What about the report, Mrs. Kronholm, that you were in the trunk of a car for eight hours?"

"That's true. They transported me from place to place. They felt their only protection was to keep me out of sight. That was a very frightening experience for me. I begged them not to put me in the trunk."

"Can you tell us what was going through your mind as this time progressed? What you thought?"

"Well, I must say that the only—the greatest—amount of things that were going through my mind was my Christian upbringing, which I'm so thankful for. Then, I kept continually feeling the presence of God the whole time and the verse that kept coming back to me

117

is, 'Thou wilt keep him in perfect peace, whose mind is stayed on thee.'

"And you know, sometimes you feel you can't control your mind, but you can. And I refused to think about the things that were ugly and the things that might happen and had happened, and well, God was good. He was just good, that's all. And he kept giving me those things, 'Be not, fear thou not, I'll be with you. Be not dismayed,' you know."

"We had a report, Mrs. Kronholm, that the kidnappers originally planned on taking both you and your husband. That your husband left for work too early and foiled the plan. Can you comment on that, please?"

"Well, that is what one of the men said. He felt that was part of the spoiling of their plan, that it would have been much easier if they could have abducted Gunnar, taken him to the bank, and explained that they had me in custody and all they had to do is to get some money and then drop it off at a certain place . . . So from all intent, I think they expected it would be over within a few hours."

"You were allowed to listen to the radio part of the time—"

Eunice told about getting KTIS on Sunday morning and listening to the service of First Baptist Church. She told of witnessing to her abductors, and her audience laughed when she related how Jerry said Billy Graham was a "pretty good preacher."

Eunice was relaxed now. She felt a rapport

with these men and women. It was getting easier to be coherent.

She told of how she had given her abductors names, how they had shared their food. "That first day I had a can of Bubble-Up and some water. And then, they had a several-day-old submarine sandwich, so they gave me about a two-inch square of that. The next day I guess it was, I asked if they had anything to eat because I was getting a little hungry, and they said, 'All we have is a dry old wiener bun.' And I said, 'Well, that's fine.' So they gave me a glass of water and the wiener bun, and I thought, well, goodness, maybe I won't get anything more, so I'd better save half of it. So I broke it in half and stuffed the other half in my coat pocket, and I had to keep some of my humor with me, I said, 'Well, bread and water, that's what they give prisoners, isn't it?' And later on I had to eat the other half of it."

"Mrs. Kronholm, can you give us a more complete accounting of how you got away—what it was you said to your abductors that caused them to let you go?"

"By this time, the tension was really building up in me. There were times when I was just so perfectly at peace that I really had no problem, but it was when they kept saying, 'Well, it will just be a few hours, it will just be a few hours,' and I knew by this time that my husband had given the money to the men and I assumed that it surely couldn't be very long before they would let me go. And I did believe that they would let me go.

"But when they didn't and they finally brought me to another place and told me to lie down on the floor again, then I knew it wasn't going to be right away.

"And by that time I was quite—shook. And it was at this time, really, that I just decided that if my Christian faith meant anything to me at all, that I've got to ask God for a specific time for a release. And six o'clock came to me and I just decided, 'God, bring me home by six o'clock tonight. I need to know that you're that kind of God, and the nation needs to know that you're that kind of God.'

"And strangely enough, I was at perfect peace at that time. I just lay down and waited and at eleven o'clock one of the abductors left to make some phone calls or something so that Jerry and I were alone."

She related the news broadcast of the arrest of "James Johnson" and her subsequent conversation with Jerry about leaving. She told of her escape.

Then the reporters asked Gunnar about the ransom and his decision to have Johnson picked up. Gunnar answered very carefully, mindful of Thor Anderson's warning, and the press conference was over.

Wednesday, Gunnar

Gunnar had made arrangements with the St. Paul Athletic Club to have a private dining room reserved for his family for dinner.

There they all gathered in a feast of thanksgiving, all the Petersons and the Kronholms.

At the close of the evening, after a wonderful meal and much giving of thanks, John, the eldest son, stood up and said, "I think it's appropriate at this time to give a toast and an ovation to the woman those courage, personality, and faith confounded her abductors. I give you Eunice Kronholm."

Everyone cried. John, a quiet and sincere man, had touched every heart with his affectionate words of admiration for his father's wife.

When Gunnar had realized he wanted to ask Eunice to be his wife, he had given much thought to how his family would accept the idea. Eunice, fourteen years younger than he, had never been married. Would she be able to include his family in their plans to the degree he would hope she would? Was she mature enough to recognize how close he was to his six grown children without being jealous or feeling left out? And they—would they accept her? Mark, still in high school, would be leaving for college the following year. Gunnar had known his own life would become lonelier as each of the children made their own future.

Now as he saw the emotion between Eunice and his children, he knew they loved each other. How he loved them all!

The next day, "Jerry" gave himself up to the FBI.

Thursday, March 21

His real name was Frederick Henry Helberg.

When Eunice had gone west to the Superette, he had gone east to a shopping center where he cashed a ten dollar bill of the $10,000 which Johnson had called their "getaway money."

He had searched for the rest of the money. That morning, he had dragged the heavy bag to the garage and set it alongside the snowmobile trailer as Johnson had directed him to.

Johnson had told him if anything went wrong, he was supposed to take the money, go about two miles into the woods, and bury it, go steal a car, and come back, get Mrs. Kronholm, and get rid of her—dump her off somewhere.

But when he went to the garage, he couldn't find the money. It had been moved.

Now he bought some cigarettes and took a cab to a Country Kitchen in West St. Paul where he had a meal. From there, he walked to a liquor store and bought a fifth of liquor, then walked to his girl friend's place.

He knocked on the door: "Hi, Dixie."

"Get out of here!" The door slammed in his face.

Fred turned and walked away. At the back of the yard was a ditch. He went down to the bottom, out of the wind, and opened his bottle. He sat there drinking until he was very cold. Dixie's house had darkened, so he decided to try the back door. Perhaps he could sleep in the laundry room. He got in and quietly stayed there for several hours. Toward morning, he stole outside again and went to sleep in the ditch.

It was cold. It reminded him of how cold he had been the night he picked up the ransom money and waited for hours for Johnson to come back and get him. That night, he had even tried to crawl into the canvas bag that said "G. E. Kronholm" on it. He had taken the money out and used the bag as a protection from the wind.

He could use something like that right now, cold as he was.

The next morning, he went to Concord Street and spent the day in a bar, then rode a bus into Minneapolis, where he continued drinking on Franklin Avenue. The bartender knew of a rooming house near by. Fred rented a room and slept in it two nights.

On Wednesday, in a bar he heard over the news that the FBI had found all except $10,000 of the ransom money under a trailer in the garage at 1204 Echo Drive in Burnsville. The papers said that a man named Fox, a carpenter, owned the house. He had helped Johnson build it.

On Thursday, after a good meal, Fred Helberg called the FBI from the Anchor Bar. As he waited for them to come, he had another drink.

123

When they arrived, they walked past him, but he waved to them. "You the FBI?"

"Yes."

"I'm Fritz Helberg." They saw a dark, square-jawed, short-haired man with black-rimmed glasses. They placed him under arrest. He gave them the money he had on him.

A week later, Helberg and Johnson were both indicted for kidnapping by the Anoka County Grand Jury. The state kidnapping charges were added to federal charges of extortion.

The following day, newspaper accounts stated that a third man, Thomas Hodgman, faced extortion charges but was not indicted for kidnapping. The papers said the FBI presumably did not consider him involved in the actual abduction of Mrs. Kronholm.

Hodgman was accused of driving Johnson and Helberg to the vicinity of the Kronholm residence and dropping them off, then later picking Helberg up in Edina.

Wednesday,
April 24,
Gunnar

Gunnar hadn't been to a Rotary Club meeting for four weeks. It was getting harder to face people. His distress today was as severe as it had ever been, but he knew he had to resume some of his normal associations.

He got through it, engaging in small talk with a few friends and acquaintances. He was glad to get back to the bank.

At 1:30, the man who had sat across the table from Gunnar, Bob McKuen, minister of Christ Episcopal Church in South St. Paul, came into the bank and into Gunnar's office.

Gunnar rose from his chair and shook hands. "Bob! Good to see you here. This is a happy surprise. What may I do for you?"

"You seemed so depressed at lunch, Gunnar." Bob's bright blue eyes usually held a twinkle but now were serious. "My own heart was weighed down for you. I'm wondering—could I be of any assistance to you? Could I pray for you?"

The compassion, the deep caring in Bob's voice and face touched Gunnar deeply. "I'm—I'm so glad—you've come. Since the kidnapping—you just wouldn't believe the lies

125

and innuendoes that have been rumored about. I find it very upsetting."

Bob waited a moment. "I see. I'm sure you do. Not that I've heard anything. No more than what's in the papers."

"The FBI has been here several times checking the last few audits done on the bank." Gunnar spoke slowly and heavily.

Bob's eyebrows shot up. "Oh? Not really! Surely they don't— You?"

"Yes. It seems the defense is trying to make it appear that I needed money and was a participant in the kidnapping."

Bob shook his head. "Whoever heard of such nonsense!"

"First they were going to broadcast over the news that I was involved in an embezzlement at the bank in the amount of $140,000. That was never broadcast—why I don't know, but, when they told me this, I told the FBI the books were open and they examined recent audits. This was and is a cause of great concern to me, not only for myself and Eunice but for the bank." Gunnar's eyes had again filled up.

"I'm sure. Yes, it would be." Bob ran his fingers through his gray hair. "How do they dare malign you like that?"

"Then a day or two later, the same agent returned, saying he was sorry, but he had to check another thing out. Again, there was a news story about to break saying I was involved in Las Vegas gambling and had suffered some serious losses and for this reason was involved in the kidnapping."

"Absurd!" Bob smiled now. "They don't know you very well, do they? That one thing is clear!"

"I told that agent I had never been to Las Vegas, was not a gambler, and that this could be verified by anyone. By this time, I was angry at these evil efforts to make a defense for the kidnapper regardless of what it might do to us. I told the FBI agent that if the radio station wanted to make that break, they might have some new owners the following morning."

Bob shook his head. "I don't blame you. Not at all."

"But that wasn't the end." Gunnar got up and began to pace the floor.

"More?"

"A week or so after that, the FBI again questioned me about whether there was any illegal loan to a Las Vegas broker. A motel was involved. That agent hated to keep coming here. He was most apologetic but it was his job. I understood that. Well, they had the information that a newsbreak was going to state that I had made some illegal loans out there and therefore was involved in the kidnapping."

"Willing to stoop to any level. That angers me, too."

Gunnar had never seen Bob's face so darkly angry. "I was, and still sometimes am, ready to resign to protect the bank. This has been my—life." Gunnar was openly weeping now. "I talked with the representative of the Majority Stockholder of the bank. I offered my resignation." He wiped his eyes and held the handkerchief over them.

"What did he say?"

"He said they had never thought of such a thing. They wouldn't consider it under any circumstances." He smiled weakly at Bob.

Bob laughed heartily. "That's not too surprising."

"It's good to talk to someone that believes in me. You begin to wonder how people *can* continue to believe in you. A few old acquaintances have even slighted me lately. I'm getting so I hate to go out."

"We've missed you at Rotary."

"That's why. It was hard for me to go today. Terribly hard."

"I could tell something was wrong. How's your wife?"

"They haven't left her alone either. Terrible rumors have been started. She was told to expect that the defense would try to make it appear in the trial that she was a willing accomplice. They might even rumor that she was Johnson's mistress before, during, and after the kidnapping." Gunnar shuddered. "She's taking all of this rather well. It distresses her, but she isn't overwhelmed by it. Eunice has a remarkable ability to see things as they are. She doesn't lose her perspective easily. She says, 'People who know me will never believe I was his mistress.' "

They both laughed. Bob said, "Of course not."

"And then, we both dread the trial coming up soon. We really need prayer. So much of the time we feel we depend on others to pray. We become so encumbered that we don't pray very well—"

The men sat together in silence. Then Gunnar said, "It's been good to talk to you, Bob. Yes, I would like to have you pray for me."

Placing both of his hands on Gunnar's head, Bob prayed that God would sustain Gunnar through further trials and show himself in peace and comfort.

As Bob prayed, the burden Gunnar had carried for weeks slipped quietly from his shoulders. For several days, he lived in the afterglow of that hour.

Wednesday,
May 8,
Gunnar

"Good night. Thanks for coming over. Yeah, we sort of dreaded coming back to the empty house." Gunnar waved to Oliver and Dorothy. To Eunice, standing in the doorway, he said, "I'll bring in the bags."

That morning, they had returned from Washington, D. C. Every year, they went there to visit Melvin and attend the convention of Minnesota Bankers. The highlight of this convention was that the bankers had opportunity to visit with the Minnesota delegation of senators and congressmen.

They had left their car at the airport on Saturday and boarded the plane. Today, when they returned, they got into their car and each had gone to work. After work, they had dinner together downtown, then attended a meeting at their church.

After church, they had asked Oliver and Dorothy to come in for coffee and to watch the news. The event everyone was talking about had occurred Saturday morning just prior to their departure.

It had come over the news as they were packing to go to Washington. James Johnson, out on bail, had been shot in the head on the freeway, had managed to drive himself off, and had crashed into a Country Kitchen before losing consciousness. Later, Johnson had told authorities a car had driven up beside him and someone had fired a shot at him.

As Gunnar set the bags in the house, he reviewed the interview with Johnson they had heard over television less than an hour ago. It seemed a case was being built for his defense. The interviewer's questions gave Johnson opportunity to hint more than slightly at the possibility that the dark underworld from Chicago had played a role in the kidnapping, and that it was they who had shot him.

Gunnar didn't like it. He stood frowning at the thumb latch on the back door. It was not engaged. But the chain lock was on the door. "John's been here to check the house. He just forgot to engage the thumb lock." Gunnar decided to investigate thoroughly.

He moved from window to window. Everything seemed in order.

True, Eunice had been frightened by the threat that others were involved, but Jerry and Bill had said the "others" were from around here and therefore didn't want to be directly involved. Eunice said she was thinking more and more that it was Bill's strategy to keep her afraid and nervous, like his telling her a policeman had been shot. She doubted if there ever were others in on it at all—either local or from Chicago.

Eunice was busy unpacking now. Gunnar felt

a force within him compelling him to keep on checking—not to stop.

He went into the furnace room. This tiny room, four by five feet, contained the electric furnace and a small trap door which opened into a crawl place under the entire house.

Gunnar was becoming aware of an increasing sense of unease. Eunice had called Joe Trimbach, Minneapolis head of the FBI, that afternoon and had told him what Clarence Kelley, director of the FBI, had said to her that very day in Washington. "Well, you've had it. So you need have no further worries about that. Never has anyone been subjected to a kidnapping twice."

To this Trimbach had said, "Just be alert anyway. Don't even walk out to your car alone when you go to and from work. Notice strange cars in your neighborhood. Watch people."

The FBI were wonderful. Gunnar had been so glad for the invitation to see Mr. Kelley and tell him what a magnificent job his agents had done in March.

As Gunnar surveyed the trap door, he noted that the two hasps by which the door is lifted were in improper position. Someone had taken the door out of the hatch, and in putting it back, had reversed the normal position of the two hasps.

Now very suspicious and sweating profusely, Gunnar opened the hatch door. *The light in the crawl space was out.* It should have come on with the light in the furnace room.

Leaving the hatch door open, he went to the

garage to get a flashlight. Hurrying back, he went into the crawl space to check the light. Gunnar pulled on the drawstring and the light came back on. *Someone had been there.*

Cold fear seized him. The need to know impelled him forward. He walked stealthily to where the crawl space formed an "L" and threw the beam of the light over there. All he saw was camping equipment and Christmas decorations. As he started back to the step to go up from the crawl space, he threw the light to the front of the area. Here was the six-foot base of the fireplace of the family room.

Two feet disappeared suddenly behind the fireplace base.

"Oh, no! We have company!" Gunnar's hair jerked in its roots. Cold clammy sweat gathered in pools all over his body.

Swiftly, he shut off the light, went to the stairway, and up through the hatch, dropping the door into place. He turned off the light in the crawl space area and hollered, "Eunice! Eunice!"

She didn't answer. He didn't hear her walking. Only silence. "Eunice!" He felt panic. Another intruder might already have gotten to her! He called again and again.

At last. "Yes, what's the trouble?" She stood peering at him.

"Get me the telephone quickly. Quick!"

She seemed frozen.

"Quick. We have company downstairs!"

Recovering fast, Eunice handed him the phone. "Do you want the gun?"

"Yes. Hurry!" Thank God, he had shown her, since the kidnapping, how to take the gun out from under the bed, and out of the case; and how to load the gun.

Gunnar dialed the operator, keeping an eye on the trap door. "This is the Kronholm residence. Get the police at once. We have—" The trap door was starting to move! "—intruders!" He had no time to give the address. He dropped the phone and Eunice handed him the gun. Jamming a shell into it, Gunnar shouted, "Look, Mister, I have a 12-gauge shotgun here and I'm going to pull the trigger unless you drop this trap door." It dropped immediately and Gunnar stood on it.

Then, fearing that the man might shoot up through the door, Gunnar beckoned Eunice to join him and they each stood on the edges of it. Eunice barely interrupted her dialing. She had telephoned Dorothy and Oliver and now was calling neighbors.

The trap door again began to wiggle. "Mister," Gunnar warned, "I'm going to blow your head off if you raise that door any further. You'd better drop it.".

Once more it dropped.

Perspiration ran down Gunnar's face and neck and back. When would help come? How much longer could he keep that man down in that hole?

Once more it started to raise slowly. Gunnar shouted, "This is your last warning. Next time, I'm going to pull the trigger without warning. So *drop that door.*" It dropped.

Relief again swept over Gunnar. Just then,

pounding at the door and the ringing of the doorbell signalled the arrival of help. Eunice raced to the door and returned with Oliver and Dorothy, several neighbors and the police.

Gunnar was shaking. "We have a visitor in the basement; whether there's more than one, I don't know, but I saw feet disappear behind the base of the fireplace. Down there." He pointed to the trap door.

"You better leave," the police said. "Go to the neighbors. We'll handle it."

Eunice, weeping, and Gunnar gratefully left. Everyone who had gathered went to the Jaworski home, four doors away, with a policeman guarding them.

There they waited. Everyone wanted to know the details. What, they wondered, did the man want? Was he part of the kidnap plot? They congratulated Gunnar for his super job of holding him at bay until the police arrived.

Gunnar, still trembling, said, "I'm so grateful that we found him. We could have just gone to bed, and then—it's the strangest thing. I had this inner voice urging me to keep checking the house even when I had earlier satisfied myself that all was well." He puckered his forehead. "Just wonder what's going on over there. It's surely taking them—"

Finally a policeman came over to the Jaworskis, dismay all over his face. "He got away."

"What?" exclaimed Gunnar. "You mean you don't have him? You let him get away?"

The policeman was obviously embarrassed. "Yup, he got away."

Gunnar was incredulous. He had held the man at bay for many minutes. Several police units had converged on the house in response to his call. Couldn't all of them together take one man? "Well, where is he? Running loose? Out there in the woods?"

Fear fell upon the neighbors assembled there.

"The only way he could have escaped was through that trap door," Gunnar insisted. "How in the world could he get away?" He just couldn't believe it.

"You'd better go to your brother's. You shouldn't stay in the house tonight."

Gunnar and Eunice readily agreed. The police hustled them out under heavy guard, and drove them to Oliver's house on the other side of the lake, with more police for escort. When they got there, the officer said, "You might as well go to bed. Take something for your nerves and try to sleep. We'll guard the house."

Oliver said, "You go to bed. I'll stay awake. I'll keep my shotgun handy and stay on guard."

"I'll fix some hot chocolate and sandwiches," Dorothy said.

"I wonder," Eunice said, "if I shouldn't call the FBI—"

"By all means," Gunnar agreed. "Call Brady."

Brady came right over and they gave him the whole story.

Thursday,
May 9

Next morning Gunnar and Eunice returned to their own house under heavy guard. Police stayed with them throughout the morning. From them, they learned how the man had got away the night before.

The police had waited at the opening to the crawl space, and hearing nothing, and receiving no response upon calling for him to come out, began to wonder if perhaps Gunnar Kronholm hadn't become overly sensitive and imagined there was someone in there. After some time the police chief of Lino Lakes went down the hole to check it out. Instantly, he got an automatic in his face. The man quickly took his gun and forced him to lie face down on the floor, then ordered his partner to come down.

He, too, went down and was also disarmed. By this time, the man was in possession of two service revolvers and a sawed-off shotgun, plus a .32 automatic pistol. Then he told the second police officer to go back upstairs to get Gunnar and Eunice.

"What for?"

"Because I need them."

The policeman went upstairs but the

Kronholms had by then gone to the Jaworskis. The officers upstairs said that under no circumstances would the Kronholms come back, so the policeman went back down into the crawl space area for the second time, this time with even greater fear.

At this point, the intruder ordered the two police in the crawl space to lie down on the floor and stay down under threat of death. He ordered all the officers out of the house and all the lights turned off. They had gone out the front door and the man escaped out the unguarded back door.

The search was on. He was a very young man, a kid, some said. The Kronholms shivered in their home, all sense of security gone. The hordes of police were of little comfort. The news carried the story about the intruder in their home the night before. Friends telephoned. They waited.

Before noon the man was captured. He had tried to fire on the FBI agents and they in turn had critically wounded him. He was about twenty years old. His name was Danny Caliendo.

Friday,
June 7,
Eunice and Gunnar

Kelley had said chances of being kidnapped twice were only one in a million. Now Eunice and Gunnar had barely escaped a second attempt. While probability of a third attempt was, no doubt, even slimmer, their sense of security was gone.

Gunnar had gone back to work a few days after he and Eunice had been discharged from the hospital. Marcia had stayed with Eunice for several weeks. Her nights were filled with bad dreams and her days characterized by fear. Try as she would, she hadn't seemed able to pull herself together staying at home.

When Gunnar suggested that it might help her to get back to work, she considered it. Marcia would watch her from inside the house as she ran outside and got in her car. She'd keep the doors locked and be careful of strangers.

Working had helped her even though fatigue never left her. The middle of each day, she would have to take a rest.

They had both begun to feel normal again. Eunice had somewhat overcome the jitters of driving alone and had started to regain her strength.

Now fear was again a constant companion to them both. Their lovely home was no longer a sanctuary but a place of dread. Relatives had stayed with them most of the time since May 8, when Caliendo had been found in their home.

They were more afraid than ever. Eunice wakened early every morning, her first thoughts always the same. As though drawn by a magnet, her mind would return to those awful moments of the abduction. She was getting very tired; her tolerance level was at an all-time low. She was tense and jumpy.

Gunnar too slept poorly. Nightmares returned over and over; he would be grappling with an intruder in a life-and-death struggle.

This evening, alone in their home, a terrible oppression of fear lay heavy about them. They jumped at the squeak of a board. "Dear God, what more can we do?" Gunnar asked, his voice thick.

"Have you taken anything?"

"I haven't—yet—" Gunnar disliked taking tranquilizers. True, the psychiatrist Eunice had been seeing, had prescribed them.

Eunice said, "I'll get you a Valium. Dr. Berry says we shouldn't hesitate to use them when we need them."

Returning to the living room with a glass of water and a pill, Eunice said, "We'll feel safer when the bank gets that security system installed here. We've done everything Dr. Berry suggested. I told you, didn't I, that Randy's pretty sure he's got a student lined up to come and live here?"

Gunnar nodded. Eunice could tell his mind was elsewhere. "Yes," he said, finally, "that will help some, having Paul here." He put Knop off his lap for the second time. "I'm especially glad for you that Paul will be here mornings when I'm not. That was a good idea Ruth had of getting a college student to live with us."

"Dr. Berry emphasized again when I saw him last Thursday that it's absolutely essential that we do everything possible as soon as possible to make this house secure. For our own peace of mind."

"We have a gun under every bed—"

"And then there's Cuddles—" Hearing her name, Cuddles shoved her nose under Eunice's hand.

For a moment, Gunnar's drawn face brightened. "Cuddles. Quite a name for a German Shepherd." Tail wagging, Cuddles was now expecting a petting from Gunnar. "You're a nice dog," he said. "She really is. She responds well." He scratched Cuddles's head and gently pulled her ears. He continued, "I liked Lawrence, too, though. We had him such a short time. Craig misses him on the farm. I wonder whatever happened to him."

"Cuddles was one of the best buys we ever made." Eunice laughed. "Ten dollars with an $8.95 bag of dog food thrown in." It made her feel better to talk about things that didn't remind her of their fear.

Gunnar was still thinking about Lawrence. "From the time we got him in March until he disappeared just a few days before Caliendo

141

moved into our crawl space, he never left home. He had been with me in the garage just before dinner—"

"And disappeared during dinner. He just wasn't to be located either."

The conversation was going wrong again. "Should I put a record on?" she asked. "What would you like?"

"It doesn't matter. A lot of strange things—our dog is stolen, Johnson is shot, Caliendo tries to kidnap us. The FBI are so sure he was just a kook that thought he could do a better job than Johnson and Helberg, and was acting alone." He paused and listened. "What was that? It's harder to listen with the record player on."

She shut it off and they both listened.

"—acting alone, they think. Came clear from Chicago to do it." Fear was again building up in them both.

"Those nightmares. If only I could get a good night's rest." Gunnar sat bent forward, his head in his hands, his glasses dangling from his fingers. He got up and began pacing the floor.

Eunice was praying. She started thinking about Irene Gifford.

A friend had reminded Eunice of Irene shortly after the kidnapping, when Eunice's nerves were at their worst. "She has a gift of prayer, a unique power of prayer. You should go to see her."

Eunice had—several times. On each occasion, Irene would question her carefully to determine what her needs were and then would pray with her. In each case, Eunice had been greatly helped.

Now Eunice said, "I don't know how I could have gotten through these last months if it hadn't been for Irene. That day at the bank, she helped you, too, didn't she? I could tell you were relieved right away."

"Yes. Yes. I wish she were here right now." He walked up and down in the living room and dining area. Then he wandered into the family room. The clock struck midnight. Its usual musical ding-dong tonight sounded ominous. Gunnar paused in front of it. Made in Finland, of birch, this clock had been brought to America by his father, and "Edward Kronholm" was engraved on the gold pendulum.

Eunice had followed him. Her sudden appearance in the door startled him.

"Oh!"

"I think I'll call Irene."

Gunnar walked ahead of her back into the living room, his shoulders bent, his head lowered. "There's something sinister. I've never had so much fear." He groaned aloud, sinking again into the chair he had sat in so much of the time when Eunice was kidnapped.

She knelt on the floor beside him. "Irene always says I should call any time, day or night. I don't really think she'll mind."

"She's probably in bed. You better not, Euny." He was pacing again. "I don't think I can go to bed tonight. I've never felt like this before."

Eunice went to the phone. "She says if she has

143

a gift of prayer it's from the Lord and for his glory. I'm going to call her. Satan's getting the upper hand over us. I feel so powerless. I just can't seem to get my prayers through. Gunnar! We need help!" Her own fear seemed to grow to overwhelming proportions as she dialed.

Irene herself answered. "I'm glad you called. Certainly, any time. I told you that." First she talked with Eunice. "Tell me as specifically as you can, what your problem is right now. What's your specific need?"

"I'm—we're—I'm so afraid. And I'm so concerned about Gunnar. We're too frightened to go to bed. We've been sitting here all evening trying to calm ourselves, but—you should see him—" She was crying.

"Have you had any reason to be afraid? Seen anything or gotten any mysterious phone calls or anything?"

"No. Nothing really. It just seems to build up in our minds. We keep hearing things but there's nothing. We haven't been sleeping well at all. We're both worn out. For one thing, one thing that may be preying on my mind, is the trial. We keep hearing what a good, I mean, shrewd lawyer the defense has, and I dread that trial so much."

Irene began to pray. She praised God for his protection over them in the past, then she prayed, "O God, again tonight, right now, place your protection around Eunice and Gunnar. Place your protection all around their house that no harm can come to them. And O God, as the trial date is approaching, help Eunice and Gunnar to commit the entire matter to you. Give them the strength to carry out their roles in the trial as they should. For your glory."

Then Gunnar came to the phone and told Irene about the oppression of fear that had taken hold of him. "It's like an evil foreboding. It's sinister. I just can't get rid of it. I don't feel I dare to go to bed."

In her prayer with him, Irene acknowledged that this oppression was from Satan and she prayed that God's strong arm would lay Satan low. She prayed again that they might both sense the near presence of God and feel his loving protection around them.

Much relieved, and again feeling safe, Eunice and Gunnar both went to bed. For the first time since she had been kidnapped, Eunice slept through the night.

Gunnar slept until the alarm went off. "I feel much better," he said. "I slept like a baby."

Wednesday, August 7

The state trial of James Johnson for kidnapping had been held in June in the Anoka County Courthouse. Helberg had pleaded guilty and had testified for the state. Johnson pleaded innocent. His attorney, in his opening statement to the jury, said Johnson admitted to everything of which the state accused him, but that he had carried out the kidnapping under duress with the understanding that Mrs. Kronholm would be a willing accomplice.

The jury acquitted Johnson. News reporters, in interviews with jury members, learned that the doubt they felt regarding Johnson's guilt was because of the element of duress introduced into the case.

Johnson had maintained that he had been forced into abducting Eunice by a man known to him only as "Mike."

In the fall of 1973, Johnson claimed, he had advertised in The Minneapolis Star for persons who might assist him in the financing of a bar and restaurant. Prior to this, he had made contacts in the Chicago area.

A week or two after this ad stopped running, he said, he received a phone call from someone he had never talked with before who had asked if he still needed financing for his bar. Johnson replied that he did and the man said he'd contact him later.

Sometime later, Johnson said, the man arranged to meet him at Mr. Nib's Bar in Minneapolis, where "Mike" proposed the kidnapping of Eunice Kronholm. Johnson claimed he said he didn't want to get involved with anything and the man told him he had nothing to worry about because she was in on it.

Later, Johnson said, they had a second meeting in a car outside that same bar. He claimed he told "Mike" he didn't want to go through with this plan. Then, he contended, "Mike" told him it was too late now and threatened him, and also made threats about his daughter.

The unsolved question of who had shot Johnson when he had been out on bail added to the doubt in the minds of the jurors. At one time during their deliberation they asked the judge to explain further the meaning of duress. His instructions were that the state should have proved Johnson was not being coerced.

When the jury had returned to the courtroom to render its verdict it looked very serious. Ron Meshbesher, Johnson's attorney, had warned Mrs. Johnson to expect the worst.

Then to the surprise of everyone, the jury returned the verdict of "Not guilty."

The news of Johnson's acquittal devastated Eunice and Gunnar. By acquitting Johnson, the jury had given support to the lies and innuendoes against the Kronholms which had been raised by the defense. Now who would believe in them?

That had been in June. Now the second trial, on the federal charge of obstruction of commerce through extortion, was also over.

Immediately after testifying, Eunice and Gunnar had gone to their cabin on the island in northern Minnesota. They had spent close to a week trying to relax with family members who had come for the trial in St. Paul and now were together awaiting the outcome. The defendants in this trial had been James Johnson and Thomas Hodgman, his nephew, driver of the car that had delivered the kidnappers to the Kronholm residence in March.

As the hour for the verdict approached, the relatives decided to go to Chisholm and wait together in the Peterson house which had been unoccupied since Mrs. Peterson had gone to live in the nursing home.

Mrs. Peterson, and her sons Keno and Melvin, her daughter Elsie with her husband John Adams, and Ruth and Wally Berg and their sons Randy and Brian had gone ahead of Eunice and Gunnar. Now, gathered in the family home, they discussed the trial, which they had all attended at least in part. Some had heard one witness and some another. Some had heard the opening statements of both attorneys. Others had heard the closing remarks to the jury.

The women were in the kitchen making coffee. "I felt so sorry for Johnson's wife. Didn't she looked peaked, though? My goodness, that poor woman—" Ruth said. "What have you got there, Elsie?"

"An alka seltzer." They watched it fizz. Elsie gulped it and made a face. "Can you imagine what she feels like? I wonder if she had any idea—and those poor children—"

"Ja, dey're da vuns to be pitied," Mrs. Peterson added from her chair at the table.

In the living room, Melvin was saying, "I still can't believe he got off scot free on that kidnap charge. What was that jury thinking of? Imagine doing something as serious as kidnapping and *admitting you did it*—then being acquitted."

"You know," Wally said thoughtfully, "I think that acquittal was almost as hard on Gunnar and Eunice as the kidnapping was." He tilted his chair back against the wall.

"Well, the slander, the innuendoes—the questions raised in court about their being accomplices—you just can't believe—it's hard to believe how people can stoop so low, isn't it?" Melvin said.

They shook their heads and studied their feet in bewilderment.

"How's that coffee coming?" Keno called to the kitchen.

Mrs. Peterson appeared in the doorway and slowly made her way to her rocker in the dining area.

"Is that coffee about ready in there, Mom?" he asked.

"Ja. Ven Euny gets here ve vill haf coffee."

"This 'Mike' thing," Melvin continued. "How did they ever convince that jury there had been a

Mike? It was just Johnson's word for it that he'd been threatened, wasn't it? How could twelve people believe that?"

Wally let his chair down with a thump. "It's my understanding they didn't have to positively believe it. The judge over that case instructed the jury that the State should have proved that the defendant was *not* under duress."

"Prove he was *not* under duress." Melvin whistled softly. "How do you prove a negative?"

"You don't."

"That's it exactly!" John exclaimed. "The whole system gives the criminal the breaks!"

"You can't," Wally continued. "The foreman, or some other member of the jury, when he was interviewed later by a reporter, said they were influenced by Johnson's words when he was shot. The police—I guess all the police on the spot didn't agree on this—but at least one said that Johnson said, 'Mike's boys did it.' And they figured that he thought he was dying at the time and would tell the truth."

"I see. A dying man doesn't lie. I get it. What do the other police claim he said?" John looked skeptical.

"At least one heard him say, 'The bitch got me.' That's cleaning it up considerably, but that's the thrust of what he said." Wally smiled. "That could have been any of the women in his life. So the jury was in doubt. They felt the state hadn't proved that there *was no Mike* involved." Once again, Wally tilted back his straight chair and looked from Melvin to John to Keno.

"Makes you wonder about the courts. How can you expect justice?"

"Yeah!" John nodded violently. "I've been thinking that for a long time."

"Well," Melvin said, "I have a hunch it's going to be different this time. I understand this Judge Devitt has a reputation for being a law-and-order judge. He may have a different idea about how to interpret some of those things. If he instructs the jury—"

"—different. Yeah, if he doesn't say the state has to prove a negative—"

"It could be a whole different ball game."

"Eunice and Gunnar just drove up," Wally informed his wife.

Mrs. Peterson, who had been dozing, opened her eyes. "Are dey here?"

"Yup." Wally turned back from the window. He checked his watch. "The judge could be giving those instructions right now."

Eunice and Gunnar came in. Eunice's eyes shone bluer than usual out of a flushed face. Her hair was blown from the wind. Gunnar looked serious, almost sad.

"Coffee's ready. We waited for you," Elsie said.

"Good." Eunice forced a smile. Her eyelids fluttered nervously. "I'll be right with you." She went into her mother's bedroom. A few minutes later, she came back, her eyes red, her hair still not combed. She thanked Elsie for the coffee and sat down next to Gunnar.

"Well, Aunt Eunice, in a few hours it will all be over and you can forget the whole thing."

"Thanks, Brian. I hope you're right." Eunice knew they were trying to bolster her.

"This time it's going to be different, Euny." Ruth smiled lovingly at her sister. "Justice is going to be done. I honestly believe that."

Eunice's eyes filled with tears. Her mouth trembled.

"Who was that blonde young woman with the big blue eyes sitting in the second row, right behind that TV artist?" Elsie asked. "Did anybody notice her? Later in the washroom—she didn't know who I was, I'm sure—she was telling the lady she was with that she prays for the kidnappers every day. I never saw her before."

Eunice had stood up suddenly, spilling her coffee. "Excuse me, I'm sorry." She was crying. Once more she retreated to the bedroom.

"Was it what I said?" Elsie whispered.

"No, I don't think so," Gunnar answered. "Maybe we could talk about something else. She's pretty tense today."

"Poor Euny," Melvin said, wiping up the coffee with his napkin. "I feel so sorry for her. You know, when we were little kids I always looked out for Euny. It just breaks my heart to see this happening to her."

"I think you've got it all, Mel," Gunnar said. "Need another napkin? O.K. Coming over from the island in the boat, she asked me if I had to go so fast. Funny thing. I wasn't going any faster than I always do, but she said it bothered her that I started out so fast."

"Is that right? Ja, poor Euny." Elsie and Ruth gathered up the cups.

"Thank you." Stretching out in his chair, Melvin asked, "Where does Helberg stand now?"

"He was told he'd get half of what Johnson gets," Gunnar said.

"And Johnson was acquitted of the kidnapping, right? And what does Helberg get on this second charge—extortion?" Melvin asked.

"He said in court he understood that federal charges would be dismissed if he testified for the prosecution. I believe as it stands, he'll get half of what Johnson gets."

"Not more than seven years, they said. Half of what Johnson gets but not more than seven years," Randy said.

"How do you feel about that?" Melvin asked Gunnar.

Gunnar shook his head. "Well, Euny seems to feel that he was a weak man sucked into crime. She's convinced that he regretted it very much and will never take part in crime again." Gunnar sat thinking for a moment, cleared his throat, glanced at the closed bedroom door, and continued. "If Johnson gets off again this time, it will mean everyone goes scot-free. Except the Kronholms. Our reputations are smeared for life. On the other hand, if Johnson gets a proper sentence—well, in that case, I'll credit Helberg for helping to bring that about. He gave the FBI a statement right after he gave himself up and testified for the state in both trials." Gunnar moved to an empty chair facing the street. Conversation continued behind him; he partly listened.

"Do you think this guy who drove them to the house—this Hodgman—knew what Johnson and Helberg were up to? Helberg seemed to think he did."

"He must have known they were up to no good." That was Randy. "He gives his uncle and another guy a ride to a remote location before sunrise and they tell him if there are police around when he comes back to just go home. I'd be suspicious, wouldn't you?"

"Sure would."

Gunnar turned slightly and looked anxiously toward the bedroom. Eunice was probably having a good cry. She'd come out feeling better. He'd leave her alone.

The voices around him continued. "Meshbesher's been claiming right along that Johnson's being tried twice for the same crime. But the kidnapping is a state charge and extortion from a bank is federal, is that it?"

"I thought they showed pretty conclusively that the bank is engaged in interstate commerce. And bringing out the fact that the insurance company paid off on a policy for extortion was good, too, wasn't it? They wouldn't have paid up if they hadn't been satisfied that the money was being demanded from the bank, would they?"

"That was the whole issue of this trial: Did they demand the money from Gunnar or from the bank?"

"That defense attorney is sharp. Did you notice how he tried to get Donovan to say it was common for the underworld to enlist the help of law-abiding citizens to accomplish some of their work?''

"No, I wasn't there when Donovan testified. Wish I had been."

"I thought that young attorney for the state—Thor Anderson—I thought he did excellent work there. He asked Donovan just the right questions so that he could set the record straight on that. He asked him, with his knowledge of organized crime, whether professional criminals would select someone outside the organization and Donovan said 'No!' "

"Then Thor asked him, 'Why is that?' and he said they would have enough knowledge within their ranks to commit crimes like kidnapping and extortion."

Yes, Gunnar thought, Thor's a good man. Gunnar knew the State was greatly concerned that Johnson be convicted this time. An attorney from the justice department in Washington had been sent to assist in this trial.

One strong witness for the state was to have been an expert flown in from California to testify about the behavior of hostages and kidnap victims. Some study being done by the Rand Corporation. Thor had said this man's testimony would show that Eunice's behavior toward her captors was quite typical of all men and women in those circumstances. Because they knew they had no control over their own lives, they tended to cooperate with their captors to help them accomplish their goals and free their victims. Many became somewhat familiar with their captors, even physical, touching, shaking hands, waving and wishing them well, etc.

"A person wonders how much of a defendant's story his attorney believes, don't you? Take Meshbesher—according to Klobuchar's column in the paper, Meshbesher was surprised at the acquittal on the kidnap charge."

"Klobuchar said he was surprised because usually when a jury finds a man not guilty they come in looking cheerful, might even smile at the defendant. This jury marched in looking very sad, and that's why Meshbesher was surprised."

Gunnar stayed partly tuned in to the lively conversation. He wished Eunice would get some rest. He idly observed a neighbor going into his house across the street. He remembered Eunice telling him of the family that lived there when she was a child. They were atheistic communists. Eunice and Melvin had played with their children and Eunice had told them about Jesus. At Christmas, since those people didn't have a tree, Eunice and Melvin would give them one and decorate it for them every year. After the children had all grown up and left Chisholm, the parents had continued to get a tree each Christmas.

Gunnar checked his watch. Five-thirty. He got up and went to the bedroom. A few minutes later, he went to the kitchen and spoke to Elsie. "Would you happen to have anything for sleep with you?"

"Sleeping pills? Sure do! For Eunice?"

"She's in pretty bad shape. She's got to get some rest."

"I'll be there in a minute. I was thinking she'd like some hot milk and butter and salt. I'll be right with you."

Gunnar returned to the bedroom. "Euny, honey, Elsie has a sleeping pill. We'd like you to take one and go upstairs where it's quiet and sleep while we're waiting."

"Sure, Euny," Elsie said. "You can't go on like this. You've got to get some rest."

Her face wet and red, Eunice didn't argue. The three of them went upstairs. She took the capsule and water from Elsie, then the hot milk. "Thank you," she whispered. "This is so good." Elsie kissed her.

Gunnar stroked her face and hair and kissed her. "I'll call you as soon as we hear anything. I'll take your cup. Try to sleep, dearest."

When Elsie returned to the kitchen, Ruth had started supper.

"Keno brought along some of his pickled fish. And he brought some *filebonk.*"

"Did he? Good! There's just no substitute for *filebonk.* Some say yogurt, but I've never tasted yogurt that compares to Keno's or mother's *filebonk.* What else is there to eat?"

"Well, Wally bought some strawberries and there's ice cream. Is there still some of that good bread? I put a ham casserole in the oven, and that about finished up the ham."

"Do you think the jury will decide tonight?" Brian asked Gunnar as he returned to the family.

"Hard to say. I surely hope so. I plan to call Thor Anderson a little later."

Still the hostess, Mrs. Peterson now called, "Komma till bord nu."

They went into the dining room. Melvin asked the blessing and then Mrs. Peterson said the traditional, "Var sã god." "Help yourself."

"Seems like old times," Melvin said. "I live for these reunions. Too bad such an unhappy occasion brought us together for this one."

"Keno, this fish is just delicious," Ruth said. "We're sure glad you brought it."

"Do you still smoke venison?" Melvin asked.

"Sure do! Whenever I get my deer."

"This fish is as good as mother's," Elsie said. "Mother, you're the best cook!"

Mrs. Peterson's face lighted up.

"I was thinking the other day," Elsie continued, "what it must have been like for you to come to this country on the boat with those two little kids."

"And not knowing a word of English," Ruth added.

"And then to have to come all the way to Minnesota. I bet you thought you'd never get here."

"Ja, dat vasn't easy. I yust vanted to come so bad. Vot else could I do?"

"We're sure glad you did, Mom." Melvin laughed. "I still sometimes think about the good times we had as kids. We had a wonderful childhood, didn't we? Do you remember those dark nights when we'd get in the boats to go to the island? Euny would. Is she sleeping?" He turned to Gunnar.

"I looked in on her just before supper and she was sound asleep."

"Euny and I were such little kids. I remember—it seemed we always got there in the dark—"

"Dad worked and we'd go after work," Keno said.

"It would be pitch dark some nights when we'd get to the lake. Other nights the sky would be full of stars and the moon would be out."

Keno said, "Do you remember the way we and the Ericksons and Kronholms—your family, Gunnar—would tie our boats together and move out into the water?"

"We'd sing!" Ruth said.

"Oh, how we'd sing. All the boats were packed. Nine in our boat—"

"Seven in ours," Gunnar added. "And the Erickson's had eight." Wiping his mouth with his napkin and standing up, Gunnar said, "If you'll excuse me, I'll run down to the pay phone and try to get Thor Anderson. He might have some news for us by this time."

At 9:30, Gunnar, himself exhausted from tension, walked for the third time to a pay phone a few blocks away and placed a call to Thor Anderson, assistant U.S. attorney, at home.

Thor himself answered. "Yes, Gunnar, I was wishing I could get hold of you. It's good news. The jury brought a verdict of guilty for Johnson."

Gunnar's feet barely touched the ground as he

sped back to the house with the news. He raced upstairs and into the bedroom where Eunice lay sleeping. "Eunice," he whispered loudly, unable to keep the excitement out of his voice. Falling down on his knees by the bed, he pulled her into his arms and buried his head in her hair. "Eunice. Eunice, darling, it's over. It's all over. The news is good."

Eunice tried to sit up.

"Guilty. The jury found Johnson guilty," Gunnar repeated.

"Did they really? Gunnar, did they?" She stood up, then sat down on the bed. "Tell me—what did you say?"

He pulled her to her feet and, weeping now, told her again. "I just talked to Thor. The trial's over, darling. Johnson was found guilty."

Then she started to cry. They both cried. "And Hodgman?" she asked.

"Not guilty. They must have thought he wasn't aware of what was going on. Thor told me the FBI are talking to a gathering of policemen tonight at the Holiday Inn and he thought they'd like to hear from us. So I promised I'd give them a call. Come on downstairs. They're all excited down there and want to see you. Ruth and Elsie are busy fixing sandwiches."

"I just noticed—I'm hungry," Eunice said. "I haven't eaten since breakfast and it's almost dark out. What time is it?"

"9:45. I bet Brady and Donovan are happy. I'm anxious to talk to them."

Eunice gave Gunnar a joyful hug before she slipped on her shoes.

Monday, February 24, 1975

Eunice and Gunnar

With trembling fingers, Eunice opened the front door to the house. "Come in, Cuddles, that's a good girl."

Coming home alone still made her nervous, but she was getting better as the year wore on.

She plugged in the coffee pot, and went through the dining room and living room. How still it was.

They were both going to be at home this evening and were eating at home. For several days, she had been reading from the transcripts of the two trials. Thor Anderson had just recently given back her leather coat and gray pants suit which had been held since her release. He also gave her twelve volumes of transcripts of the trials.

She put her purse down on the bed and pulled a comb through her hair. She washed her hands carefully in the bathroom, then proceeded to the kitchen to start dinner.

Last night she hadn't slept much. She had read, and learned for the first time, exactly what the defendant's attorney, Mr. Meshbesher, had said in his charges to the juries.

It had been worse than she had gleaned from

those who had been there. Such simple things as the change in the hour of her hair appointment were used to make her appear the willing accomplice to the kidnapping. Their calmness and faith was ridiculed. The unsaved mentality—that was it.

She took out the beef and her electric fry pan. She wondered if she should read any more in those transcripts. "I just want to know, that's all," she said, as though defending her rights in court.

She stirred the meat. She would cook the rice and add the sour cream when Gunnar—

There he was. She heard his key in the door.

He kissed her and looked in the pan. "What's it going to be?"

"Beef stroganoff."

"Good. We haven't had that for a long time."

During dinner, they discussed the transcripts. "Well, have you learned anything new?" he asked.

"Yes—some. It makes me nervous, reading about it. Tonight I want to read you the charge Judge Devitt made to the jury in the extortion trial."

"And then I hope you will be able to start to forget—"

"*Start* to forget. Yes, it will be a while before I can put it all out of my mind."

Gunnar put "Joy Is Like the Rain" on the stereo as Eunice carried their coffee into the living room.

"I found it interesting—the remarks Thor and Meshbesher made to the jury. Like here," she opened a volume, checking the number on the front. "Thor tells them about duress: '. . . listen carefully to Judge Devitt's instructions on duress. He'll tell you, in his own words, as he thinks the law is . . . that in order to avail one's self of this duress defense, a person has to have had no reasonable opportunity to withdraw from a criminal scheme.' "

She looked up at Gunnar for a moment, then continued, tracing the sentences rapidly with her finger. " 'Five months. How much longer a reasonable opportunity can a person have?' "

"Good," Gunnar exclaimed.

"And then, farther along here he talks to them about—let's see, here it is, about the 'Mike' story. Thor still speaking here, 'Another thing: I guess what he'd like you to believe is underworld characters in this big organized crime shot him. I suppose that's the implication he'd like to leave you with. It's strange that that kind of a person would miss. It's strange that whoever did it botched it up. That's all we know about the person that did it—that they did a lousy job.' " Eunice and Gunnar both chuckled. "And then Thor said, 'And I'm very grateful for that, and I'm sure Mr. Johnson is. But this is inconsistent with the theory that all these professionals are getting their hands in this.'

"Then here he says he thinks the government has proved its case beyond a reasonable doubt. And in this volume I think it is where Devitt explains reasonable doubt to the jury." She lifted Volume VI and found a marker she had placed in it earlier. "Yeah, here. He says, 'It is not required that the government prove guilt beyond all *possible* doubt. The test is one of *reasonable* doubt. A reasonable doubt is a doubt based upon reason and common sense, the kind of doubt that would make a reasonable person hesitate to act. Proof beyond a reasonable doubt must, therefore, be proof of such a convincing character that you would be willing to rely and act upon it unhesitatingly in the most important of your own affairs.' "

"How does he define duress?"

"That's here." She found another marker. "First he went on for several pages here telling what the indictment said and explaining what extortion, and interstate commerce, and—ah—wilful intent meant—"

"What does he say about that?"

"Wilful intent?"

"Yeah."

"That's back here. Let's see. 'An act is done wilfully if it is done voluntarily, and intentionally and with the specific intent to do something the law forbids. That is to say with bad purpose either to disobey or to disregard the law.' He says since we can't look into a person's mind we have to 'judge the presence or absence of this required intent by a person's actions, by his conduct, by what he says and by what he does not say. Of course, in this case, the government argues that the criminal intent is manifest from what the defendants did. And of course, the defendants argue that criminal intent is not present and has not been shown.' "

"O. K. Now about duress."

"That follows.

" 'Four specific requirements of this defense must appear. In order to provide legal excuse for criminal conduct by the defense of coercion, there are four essentials:

" 'Number 1. The coercion to act must be present at the time.' " Eunice looked up at Gunnar, then continued slowly.

" 'Number 2. The danger must be immediate—a fear of future danger to life or body is not sufficient to relieve an accused of responsibility.

" '3. The coercion must be of such a nature as to induce a well-founded fear of impending death or serious bodily injury, and

" '4. There must be no reasonable opportunity to escape the compulsion without committing the crime; or to say it otherwise, that there is no reasonable alternative to committing the crime—you can't run away, you can't call the police, you can't do anything except commit the crime.' "

Gunnar said, "I bet Meshbesher was cringing while the judge gave those instructions. But he probably knew it was coming."

"But listen to this. He uses the case of Patricia Hearst. Kind of funny. Speaking of Meshbesher, I bet he wished he hadn't brought up *that* case because he gave the judge a good example of coercion. Look at this: Devitt speaking. 'When Mr. Meshbesher brought up the situation of Patricia Hearst, who was allegedly kidnapped months ago, you know, and then a few months later one of these bank cameras took a picture of

165

some bank robbers, and there was Patricia Hearst—you maybe saw it—with a gun and over some distance from her was the leader of the Symbionese Liberation Force, and it appeared, from the picture, that the leader of the band had the gun pointed on Patricia Hearst. And there was speculation as to whether or not she was actually participating or whether or not she was an unwilling victim, whether she was being coerced or whether she was under duress.' "

"Perfect," Gunnar grinned appreciatively. "If the first jury had had instructions like those, Johnson would never have been acquitted of kidnapping either."

"No, he sure wouldn't have!"

Gunnar sat quietly thinking, swinging his glasses. "So Johnson got twenty years in a federal prison and Hodgman went free because the jury felt he was quite innocently driving his uncle around."

"And Jerry. I mean Helberg. I was surprised that Judge Thoreen sentenced him to seven years at Stillwater. I wonder how much of that he'll have to serve. I felt he regretted his part in it."

"I told you about the day I bumped into him in Thor's office off the court room. Quite a thing to meet a man who kidnapped your wife." Gunnar's voice had grown husky. "He put out his hand to me and said, 'I'm Fritz Helberg. I can't tell you how sorry I am for all the sorrow I put you through.' " Gunnar was struggling to get control of himself. "I was speechless. I took his hand, I remember, but I'm not sure what

166

reply I made. He had no idea—no idea what it had been like." Gunnar's voice broke. "No one who has never gone through it knows what it's like. If they had any idea what they put the family through, no criminal would ever commit that crime. That's the worst there is." Taking out his handkerchief, Gunnar held it over his eyes.

Eunice was deeply moved to see Gunnar so affected. She went to him and kissed his forehead. "They don't realize—" her voice sounded thin—"Helberg didn't realize at the time what it was like. Later, he seemed to have some idea how you'd suffered. I still pray for him. I believe God's going to save him. And I—I pray for Johnson, too."

Gunnar blew his nose and put his handkerchief back in his pocket. "There was a lot of prayer going up at those trials. One big prayer meeting. I felt the support of our Christian friends there, too, just as we have through this whole thing."

"All those Christians praying for justice without a spirit of vengeance. Just that justice be done."

"And now. Do you feel it has been?" Gunnar asked.

"Well, yes and no. I still have questions about Caliendo and Hodgman. I hope five years in a prison psychiatric ward is all Caliendo needed. I have no doubt that he needs help, but I hope he'll be cured of ever pulling anything like that again."

Gunnar nodded.

Eunice continued, "The FBI is sure Caliendo wasn't connected with the original plot —that he was just a kook—and Hodgman may have known more than he admitted to, but I'm not too sorry he got off. He made a terrible mistake and I hope he learned from it. I'm sorry Johnson was acquitted of the kidnapping. That's most unfortunate. But, you remember, that night at Lake Vermillion, when we heard the first verdict, even in my despair it seemed God was telling me something good would come of it. I still have to believe that. He gave me the verse, 'Vengeance is mine. I will repay, saith the Lord.' "

A second record dropped into place on the turntable. Gunnar stood up and stretched, and loosened his tie. "I don't suppose we'll ever know exactly what influenced the juries most. I wonder if that expert from Rand influenced the second jury to any great extent."

"I came across his testimony today and was impressed. That's quite a research project the Rand Corporation is doing. Close to a dozen people have worked on that study for, well, this Mr. Ronfeldt had worked on it for a year."

"Do you recall just what he said about behavior of kidnap victims?"

Eunice reached for the transcripts.

"No, you don't have to look it up now. Do you remember?"

"It was pretty much what Thor expected. Of sixteen hostages—most of these were diplomats and other government officials kidnapped abroad by terrorists, etc.—of the sixteen interviewed by the group, Mr. Ronfeldt had personally interviewed five and had seen the transcripts of all the others. They brought in psychiatrists to review their approach and findings. They found most of the victims cooperated with their captors. Mr. Ronfeldt explained that normally a person has some feeling that he has some control over his life. That's all gone when he's kidnapped and so he's trying to help the captor get what he wants so he'll let him go. You should read it. It's interesting. I know I was acting out of fear for my life. It's interesting that so many others have reacted the same way in similar circumstances."

"I'll have to read that. That may have had quite an influence on the case."

"Thor handled the case well. I never realized before how well he had done."

"But he can't erase the innuendoes and slanderous things rumored about us and brought into the trial by the defense. There will always be people who will wonder if you were in on it, or if I was, or both of us," Gunnar said.

"But a lot of people believed in us through it all."

"Like Jim Klobuchar. How welcome his columns were from time to time. A one-man effort to keep the record straight." Gunnar was gently pulling his left ear, a mannerism Eunice always noticed.

"We might not have been quite so candid with him if we'd known he was going to tell the world exactly how we felt after the acquittal." Eunice chuckled.

"I was a bitter man for a long time," Gunnar admitted.

"But the Lord has healed our bitterness too, hasn't he?" Eunice studied him. She remembered the times they had gone together to Irene Gifford for prayer. One time they had met with her and her minister in Shakopee. This minister had told Gunnar, "As evidence of what God is going to do for you, he will relieve you of the tension and pain in your shoulders and neck before you get home." And he had.

"Just lately," Eunice said, "I've started feeling more like myself again. This has been some year!" She stacked the twelve volumes of transcripts in two piles.

"Yesterday at lunch Bob said, 'Gunnar, this is the first time you've talked banking at lunch for months.' "

"You're sleeping better, too, aren't you? I haven't had a nightmare for I don't know how long."

"Oh, yes. Feeling more like my old self every day." Gunnar paused reflectively, "I still sometimes think of the narrow escape we had that night when Caliendo was in the basement. I'm absolutely convinced we would have both been kidnapped and killed after he got the money. He was prepared with the ransom notes and the ropes and being mentally in need of help, I feel—I guess I can't forget the way a force outside of myself just wouldn't give me peace about checking the house that night. I know it was the Lord keeping me at it until I discovered him."

Eunice went over to where he sat. The strains of "Sheep May Safely Graze" came from the stereo. She sat on his lap and put her head on his shoulder. "God has been good. Really, when I think of how he protected us and kept us, I feel we are really in his hands and *nothing* will happen to us that he doesn't allow."

He held her close. "So many people, all those testimonies from all over the world, still coming in, of how their faith was strengthened. Some were even saved because of this thing. God's ways truly are not our ways—"

The telephone rang. Eunice took it in the bedroom. "It's Dorothy," she called to Gunnar. "They want us to come over for coffee."

"Tell her we'll be right over." He met Eunice in the center hallway and drew her to him in a long, tender embrace.